WHEN THE BLACK

WHEN THE BLACK GIRL SINGS

Bil Wright

Simon & Schuster Books for Young Readers
New York London Toronto Sydney

SIMON & SCHUSTER BOOKS FOR YOUNG READERS
An imprint of Simon & Schuster Children's Publishing Division
1230 Avenue of the Americas, New York, New York 10020
This book is a work of fiction. Any references to historical events, real people, or real locales are used fictitiously. Other names, characters, places, and incidents are products of the author's imagination, and any resemblance to actual events or locales or persons, living or dead, is entirely coincidental.

Book design by Kristin Smith
The text for this book is set in Giovanni.
Manufactured in the United States of America
2 4 6 8 10 9 7 5 3 1
Library of Congress Cataloging-in-Publication Data
Wright, Bil.
When the black girl sings / Bil Wright.—1st ed.
p. cm.
Summary: Adopted by white parents and sent to an exclusive Connecticut girls' school where she is the only black student, fourteen-year-old Lahni Schuler feels like an outcast, particularly when her parents separate, but after attending a local church where she hears gospel music for the first time, she finds her voice.
ISBN-13: 978-1-4169-3995-5 (hardcover : alk. paper)
ISBN-10: 1-4169-3995-4 (hardcover : alk. paper)
[1. Identity—Fiction. 2. Interracial adoption—Fiction. 3. Singing—Fiction. 4. African Americans—Fiction. 5. Divorce—Fiction. 6. Connecticut—Fiction.] I. Title.
PZ7.W9335Wh 2007
[Fic]—dc22
2006030837

ACKNOWLEDGMENTS

The author wishes to thank Bill Engel, Helen Thomassen, Becket Logan, Melody Baker, Cherise Davis, and Ms. Regina Brooks.

Also to Lia Ubl and Leah Russell Novak for their insights and generosity.

To my family: Traci, Robynne, Ravae, Jerry, Karen, Paul, Max, Franz, Kyle, and Sean.

Much gratitude to David Gale for being so good at what he does and Alexandra Cooper for her sensitivity and diligence.

CHAPTER ONE 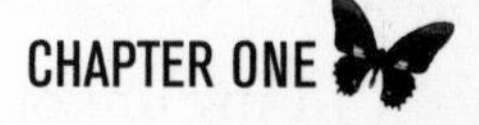

I never once let any of them see me naked. Until that Friday, when I had no choice.

We'd just had gym. I finished taking my shower, stuck my arm out from behind the green plastic curtain, and reached around to the towel rack. I was still humming the song I'd made up in the shower, hoping I could keep the words in my head until I got to my notebook and a pen.

No towel. I poked my head out to see if maybe it had dropped on the floor. Not there, either.

I stepped out of the shower stall and walked to my locker, trying to look like I was as comfortable naked as Amber Merrill or Chrissie Lamb or especially Donna Thoren. They all pretended it was totally natural to put on blush and lip gloss before they put on underwear. For me, it was always from my towel to my clothes. No conversation with anyone until I was dressed.

When I couldn't get my locker open, my hands started to shake and I couldn't remember the combination. I stopped humming. I tried not to think about whether anyone was watching me, but I knew they must be. I never let any of them see me like that—dripping wet in front of my locker, turning the dial round and round and back again.

In my uniform, they saw my face, neck, arms, knees, and legs. All the other parts they liked to gossip, snicker, or brag about, they couldn't usually see on me.

I didn't talk about shaving under my arms or the hair on my legs, which I didn't have. I didn't compare the size or the shape of my breasts with any of them. When one of the girls tried to talk to me about those things, I gave her this look that said, *Let's not go down that road!* It was what my mother said when she absolutely didn't want to discuss something. I tried to look like she sounded when she said it.

Standing there naked in front of my locker, I could feel them staring. Not Donna Thoren, of course. Donna was sitting on the bench between the rows of lockers. She was nude, as usual, looking in the mirror and saying, "I can hardly brush my hair anymore, these things are getting so big." Being in the locker room always meant seeing and hearing about Donna's breasts. There was no way to avoid it unless you were stone-deaf. Her breasts seemed to be what she liked to talk about more than anything besides her boyfriend, Jeff Krieger. Katie Frankenfeldt, my best friend, had cracked just two days before, "She treats those things like pets. She should just name them and buy collars for them."

Today, Donna Thoren stopped talking about her breasts long enough to look up at me dripping and spinning the dial. "Whooaa!" she called out. Then she said loudly in a deep voice, "The Explore Channel presents *A Visit with Our African Neighbors*!"

My fingers froze on the lock. Water ran down my forehead and under my arms. My bare skin was chilled. I knew I had no choice.

"What is that supposed to mean?" I looked at her over my shoulder, trying to pretend I wasn't making a pitiful attempt to cover myself with my skinny, dark brown arms and elbows. I wanted to sound tough, as though I would beat her head in if she didn't watch her mouth.

But Donna Thoren wasn't capable of watching her mouth. By now all the girls in the locker room had stopped to listen.

"Oh, get over it!" Donna smirked. "I was just teasing

you." She shrugged. "Besides, without any clothes on, you *do* look like one of those little black African babies you see on TV specials. Except your stomach isn't sticking out, so I guess you're not starving."

As Katie would say, Donna was definitely just begging to have her butt kicked.

Most of the girls laughed like they thought Donna should have Jay Leno's job on the *Tonight Show*. A few of them got dressed really fast so they could watch what would happen. But they also wanted to be able to get out in a hurry if there was a big fight and a teacher came in to break it up. It didn't happen often at The Darby School, but when it did, the teacher usually punished any girl who happened to be in the room. It was supposed to teach you that if you thought something was wrong, you shouldn't have been standing there watching.

I wanted to turn around and face Donna directly, to say something really evil and hurtful. But nothing would come to me. So I said over my shoulder in the most condescending tone I could manage, "You're so freakin' ignorant, Donna. You and your stupid breasts."

When there was absolute silence, it was pretty clear I'd scored a minus zero on the evil and hurtful scale. It seemed whenever I did my best to sound like the snappy, smart-mouthed black girls on television, I wound up sounding like the wimpiest white girl at Darby.

Katie came in from the other room, where the sinks and toilets were. Our lockers were next to each other. She handed me her towel and whispered, "forty-three–seventy-five–thirty-six." We were supposed to have memorized each other's combinations in case of an emergency. I had hers on a piece of paper somewhere in my backpack, but I hadn't memorized it.

I wrapped her towel around me, which I knew looked weird to some of the other girls, but I didn't care. By that time, I felt like they could see every pore, every scar from where I'd fallen down when I was younger. I wanted to be covered up so badly, I would probably have gone back into the shower and stayed there until they all left if Katie hadn't loaned me her towel.

Donna stood up and slowly finished getting dressed. When she finally put on her bra, she sighed and said, "I don't know what you're so ashamed of, Lahni. Some boy from Kent asked me just the other day what the black girl in my class looked like without any clothes on, and I said I had no idea. Now I can tell him that as far as I could see, everything is where it's supposed to be."

By that time I had my underwear and skirt on. My hair was still sopping wet. Water was running down onto my face. I grabbed Katie's towel again to dry it. "I'm not ashamed, Donna. I just don't think it's necessary to sit around in public half naked."

Donna started toward the sinks. The other girls had lost interest. They knew there wouldn't be any big fight. There wouldn't be that much to gossip about unless somebody made up something that hadn't happened. Donna called back into the locker room, "I know you're dying to know who the boy was, Lahni. I'll see if I can find out his name for you."

Katie and I left and went to the cafeteria for lunch. We sat at the end of a table, leaving a lot of distance between us and the other girls. I knew Katie was watching me, but she hadn't said anything except "let's go eat" when we left the locker room. Now that we were in the cafeteria, I figured she'd have some opinion about what had happened with Donna. Katie almost always had an opinion. Even if she made it up right on the spot, she always made sure you heard it. Finally I said to her, "So go ahead. I know you have just the perfect thing I should have done. What is it?"

Katie scowled and answered, "Nope. Not a thing. I was just gonna . . ."

"What? I knew it. What?"

"It's not about that. It isn't."

I didn't believe her for a second. "Yes, it is. What do you think I should have said?"

"I told you, Lahni, it's not about that. I was just gonna ask you if you have any idea who asked Donna what you look like without any clothes on."

"She was lying." I snapped my eyes open and shut at the ridiculousness of it. "She made it up."

"No way." Katie shook her head till her reddish brown bangs flopped over her eyes. She quickly parted them and flipped them up again. "Donna Thoren may be a liar, but she wouldn't lie about a boy asking how any other girl looked besides *her*. I betcha."

I stopped listening. I was sure it was a lie, and even if it wasn't, I didn't care. All I could think about was standing there naked and Donna saying I looked like a starving African baby. "I can't wait until today is over," I told Katie. "I can't wait to get out of this place."

"Why? What are you doing when you go home?"

If we were as close as Katie liked to think we were, she would have understood. Wouldn't she have wanted to be anywhere but there? Wouldn't she have wanted to never be in a locker room naked again with seventeen white girls, all of them studying you like you were a lab rat? No, I guess Katie Frankenfeldt wouldn't have understood. No matter how close she thought we were, she didn't have a clue.

"Huh?" She asked again. "What are you going to do when you get home?"

"It doesn't matter, Katie. The point is I'll be out of The Darby School. I'm so sick of these people I could scream."

Katie looked at me, struggling to come up with an answer. She probably heard from the way I'd said, "these people" that I'd meant her as much as anyone, and I could see that it hurt her. But in that moment, it was true. All I wanted to do was get out of there and away from all of them.

By the time I got home, I was fuming. "Why Darby?" I asked my mother as soon as I'd walked in. "Why couldn't I have gone to a regular public school with all different kinds of kids?"

"Because your father did research on it and thought The Darby School was a good school with a good record."

"Well, I'm tired of it. And I'm tired of those ridiculous girls."

My mother was sitting in her bedroom on the floor with clothes spread around her like her dresser had exploded. She looked up at me with her hands full of T-shirts and shorts.

"What happened to you today?" she asked calmly.

Of course, now I didn't want to repeat any of it. I didn't want to give Donna Thoren that much credit as to repeat the story and let my mother know how idiotic I had looked in front of my whole class. But I'd been the one to come in ranting, so I figured I had to come up with something. When I told her, I left out Donna's lie about the boy who'd asked her what I looked like without clothes on. Besides being a lie, it wasn't the point. The point was I was sick of The Darby School and its snooty white girls.

I finished my story about the locker room. My mother said quietly, "Maybe she meant it as a compliment."

I couldn't believe Mom was serious. "That I look like an African baby from a television special? You think she meant that as a *compliment*?" Why was it whenever I thought there was a situation that deserved for her to be just as upset as I was, she never was?

"Lahni, all I mean is that you have a lovely body with beautiful brown skin. And your hair is natural and not straightened."

"And I'm not going to straighten it either. But that still doesn't make me anybody's African baby." My hair again. It wasn't that I thought my hair was one of my best features. Or that I thought my Afro puffs were all that flattering, either. Styling my own hair wasn't exactly a great talent of mine, so Afro puffs were the best I could come up with. I wore them on top of my head or on the sides or in back. I'd tried one style for a while with a giant puff in the back and a smaller one in front, but Katie and I agreed I looked like a poodle walking around in a Darby uniform, so I stopped wearing that style to school, at least.

Because my mother was white, I didn't expect her to be good at taking care of a black girl's hair. She'd been the one to come up with a hundred variations on the Afro puff, so I had to give her some credit. But I'd never wanted to straighten my hair, no matter how tired I was of the puffs, and I wasn't going to braid it down, either. I loved that my hair was so different from the other Darby girls' hair. Anything that separated me from them was definitely worth it.

Eventually the conversation between my mother and me came back to one we'd had before. It seemed every time something that made me furious happened at Darby, I'd ask the same questions. I always wondered if my mother would answer them any differently than she had the last time. "I still don't get why you wanted a black baby. Did you ever think that maybe it should have been a Chinese baby, or why not a *white* one? It seems to me a white baby would have made a lot more sense. Two white parents sending their daughter to a white, private girls school in New Clarion, Connecticut, would definitely make more sense than two white parents sending a black girl there."

"Oh, for goodness' sake, Lahni. We are not going down that road again. Not now. Please." Sometimes she was in the mood for it, sometimes she wasn't.

"But I want you to explain to me again why you picked *me* to adopt! Whose idea was it—yours or Dad's? Didn't you think you'd be asking for a lot of trouble, considering you didn't know anything about black kids?"

"Lahni, it's not as though I haven't said this to you. Neither one of us knew anything about kids at all. The only thing we knew was that we wanted one." She looked down and started to refold one of the T-shirts she'd already folded. "We were . . . surprised . . . and . . . very . . . disappointed that I couldn't have a baby, but it didn't stop us from wanting one. We didn't care what color it was. I loved you the second I saw you. And no, I never once thought I'd be asking for trouble." My mom stopped folding and looked at me like a shy, young girl. "What I thought was, 'This beautiful little person is smiling at me. Maybe she likes me too.' Now, does that answer the 'why me?' part, at least for today?"

I nodded. It was true. She'd said it before. And each time it made sense. Until something else happened, usually at school, and I got mad and wanted to hear it all again.

"Lahni Schuler, we're in this together. You're my kid. So if you've got trouble, I've got trouble. I'm not afraid of it, Lahni. Believe me."

Actually, it was very odd to hear Ursula Schuler talking about trouble. She was pretty and soft looking. Her skin was olive beige. Her voice was deep, I thought, for a woman's. It was never high and screechy like mine could be. But that afternoon in my parents' bedroom, when my mother talked about trouble, her voice was lower than I'd ever heard it. And when she told me to believe she was not afraid of it, I did.

What bothered me was that she sounded like she knew for sure trouble was coming. And it was much bigger than Donna Thoren saying I looked like an African baby on a television special.

CHAPTER TWO 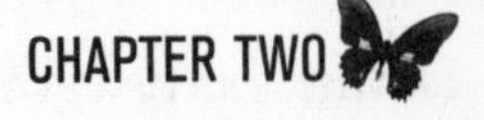

In the beginning, I admitted that I was adopted if the subject happened to come up. But I also said, if someone asked for details, that my adopted father was black. To me, it seemed easier than telling a group of white girls that two white people had adopted me and having to answer a lot of questions I'd already asked my parents and *still* didn't really trust the answers to.

I got away with lying about my father being black in the beginning because they never saw him. He always missed parent-teacher night because that was in March, and in March he was always at the same computer conference in Germany. He was never at the parent-student assemblies because they were in June, and in June he was usually back in Germany for more conferences. It wasn't until graduation from lower school that a lot of the girls saw him for the first time.

Of course, I didn't think about my lie when we were all onstage during the ceremony. I looked out at both my parents and smiled, just happy that they were there together. I never even thought about anyone remembering that I'd lied about what race my father was.

After the ceremony Mrs. Surloff, the dean, was telling my parents how glad she was I would be back in the fall. Amber Merrill called for me to come over to where she was standing, across the lawn with Katie, Donna Thoren, and Cyndi Meadows. I remember as I got closer to the three of them, Katie was trying to tell me something with her eyes, but I couldn't understand what it was. As soon as I got to them, Amber asked me, "Is that your mother and father you were standing next to?"

"Yeah," I answered her cautiously. I knew something important was about to happen.

"Why does your father look so *white*? Didn't you say he was black?"

I knew Amber was saying that I'd lied, and they were waiting for an explanation. An explanation, I decided, they would never get. If I'd said he was part Puerto Rican and part Irish setter, I wasn't going to explain why to them.

"He *looks* white because he is." I said it as though I had no memory at all of saying anything else. "He *is* white." And I turned around and walked back to where he and my mother were standing.

I took my father's hand. It was something I'd done for as long as I could remember, hold hands with my dad. It didn't matter where we were, and I wasn't even embarrassed about it as I got older. If other people stared, either I didn't notice or I didn't care. Wherever we were, at the mall or just driving along the highway, either he took my hand or I took his. We were buds, that's just the way it was.

That graduation day, when I went back across the Darby lawn and took my father's hand, I knew it probably made me look like I was about four years old to the other girls, but I didn't care. I knew they were watching. I wanted them to know there were things about my family they didn't understand and probably wouldn't ever, and that was fine by me. I was proud of us.

On my wrist was a thin braid of gold with six tiny pearls on it. My father had brought it back from his business trip and told me it was my graduation present. He'd leaned down to put it on me, and I'd kissed him on the forehead.

For the next couple of years in middle school, I would take out my bracelet from him and remember the first time I wore it. If I'd been ashamed that day of lying at all, it was because at that moment everything about my father seemed perfect. I didn't know why I'd ever said he was anything different from what he was.

CHAPTER THREE

Now, three years later, I was getting ready for another Darby graduation, this time from middle school. Everyone around me was going crazy, and they seemed determined to take me with them.

My mother and father barely got along. My father was hardly ever at home, and when he was, it seemed as though he couldn't wait to pack and get away again. He actually started leaving his suitcase in his study open and half-unpacked, so I always knew it was just a matter of hours before he was leaving. I didn't blame him, I guess. It was as though my mother had decided, *Okay, you want to act like a stranger, then I'll treat you like one.* I don't know what happened after they closed the door to their bedroom, except for the arguments.

Before this, they would call me in there with them. Sometimes we all watched a movie on television together, in bed. My father would do silly things like pretend he didn't have enough room and roll out onto the floor. He'd moan, "I broke my leg! I broke my leg! I can't go back to work for at least six months!" My mother and I would yell, "Yaaaay! Yaaaay!" Then he'd laugh and say, "You two are out of your minds! If only it was that easy!"

Or my father and I would sing for my mom. He'd use the broom for a microphone and I'd use the mop. We'd sing in harmony, usually some song we'd both heard on the radio or television. He had lots of CDs of duets in his car, and he'd play one at home and say, "Lahni, you know The Schulers can do better than that. Listen Ursula. You tell us who sounds better, Rod Stewart and Diana Ross or Tim Schuler and Lahni Schuler? Tell us we can't do that song better!"

I'd do Diana Ross's part and he'd do Rod Stewart's. Mom would laugh, and no matter what we sounded like, she'd say, "You're absolutely right, Tim. No contest. I don't know why they let the two of them sing that at all with the two of you around." I think it hurt my dad's feelings that my mom didn't really think he had a good voice. "It's a good thing for me I've got you, Lahni," he'd say. "Without you, I wouldn't have a chance for a career in show biz."

By eighth grade, it felt as though I'd dreamed up our singing days. Now it felt like my father hardly said anything much to me except, "I'll try to be home soon, pumpkin," as he was headed out the door.

My parents weren't the only ones who'd lost their minds. The girls in my class were sex crazy. All they ever talked about were "wieners" and "doing it." No one would admit to having "done it," but girls like Amber Merrill and Cyndi Meadows bragged about how many boys had begged them to. If you believed Amber, at least six boys were walking around feeling suicidal because she'd said no to them.

The middle school mixer coming up made everything worse. On June 10, the eighth grade girls from Darby and the eighth grade boys from Kent were all invited to the annual Kent-Darby middle school mixer. Once we were in upper school, most of our classes would be coed and the mixer was supposed to be the official beginning of socializing with the Kent boys.

The only thing separating Kent from Darby was a fence dividing the two schools' athletic fields. By now, it was as though the fence had completely disappeared. If the boys weren't sneaking around the Darby building, girls were getting suspended for being caught in Kent's parking lot during school hours. Or worse.

Donna Thoren claimed to know most of the boys in Kent's eighth grade and some of the boys in upper school, too. Her brother, Dirk, had been a big soccer hero at Kent. "They used to just want to go out with me because of Dirk, but now all they do is look at these"—her breasts again—"and those boys are practically standing in line over there." Katie said they were probably waiting in line to slap her because she was so obnoxious.

I'd seen boys around Kent that I thought were cute, but I guess I felt kind of invisible because for one thing, there were only three black boys at Kent—two were about to graduate from upper school and one was in lower school. The only other girl who I think felt as invisible as me was Lisa Shin, a Korean girl. It was totally ridiculous that Lisa would feel invisible because she was probably the most beautiful girl in the eighth grade. But every time the other girls started fantasizing out loud about who they wanted to date or who might ask them to the Kent-Darby middle school mixer, Lisa and I were the only two who never said a word.

Actually I didn't have any fantasies, because I never planned to go to the mixer. Eventually, I figured, I'd have a boyfriend, or a date, at least. If it didn't happen in time for the mixer, that was a matter of circumstance. What did I expect? I was a black girl at a school for white girls who wanted to date white boys. As far as I knew, Kent was basically full of white boys who were looking for Ambers and Donnas and Chrissie Lambs. For the night of the mixer, I was perfectly happy to rent a movie and stay at home.

We were running laps at the end of gym class when Donna Thoren called to me, "Lahni, there's your guy."

I looked over. So did about six other girls who'd heard her. Donna was looking in the direction of three sweaty boys sprinting across the Kent field in gym shorts and sneakers.

"The one with the skinny legs," she said. "And the red high-tops. He's the one who's dying to know what you look like naked."

I'd been close to the lead, but now I slowed down. I was both embarrassed and curious. It had been almost three weeks since Donna first made the announcement. Now she was actually identifying the guy, and there was no way I wasn't going to look up to see who it was.

Katie caught up with me and so did Donna. "I bet you thought I made it up, didn't you?" Donna laughed, practically out of breath. "But that's him, right next to Brad Tarleton. Hey, Brad!" she called suddenly. If I'd been able to sink into the athletic field, I would have. Of course, all of the guys looked over, including Mr. Red High-tops. We saw each other and he looked surprised, as though we knew each other but he hadn't expected to see me.

I looked away immediately, but then I looked back. The expression on his face was so odd, I couldn't help but be curious and get a second look.

He hadn't stopped staring. Not losing any of his speed, he was even farther ahead of the other two than he had been, but he was focused on me. His face was long and thin, and his hair was brown and curly, wild looking. He looked at me as though he was saying something to me, but I turned my head.

"You see? You see how he was checking you out?" Donna yelled. Katie grunted, "She's such a moron," but I didn't answer either one of them. I was running faster, to leave both of them behind. I wanted to go to the locker room and get dressed before anyone else came in. Most of all, I wanted to stop thinking about the boy in the red high-tops telling me something with his eyes I didn't think I wanted to hear.

CHAPTER FOUR

"How would you know what she needs? You haven't spent more than twenty minutes with her in six months!"

"You're exaggerating, Ursula. As usual. To avoid what the real issue is here."

"The real issue is she's got one parent making all the decisions. If she's thinking she needs to be around kids who are more like her—"

"Then what? We should pull her out of a good school and put her in a public one where she can be mediocre and feel good about it because more people *look* like her?"

I sat in the kitchen, supposedly making a sandwich but really only listening to them upstairs. My father had come in from the airport that night and immediately started in on all the things he said were falling apart while he was away. When Mom told him about me being angry that I was at Darby, he blew up.

What I'd never heard before was the part about me being around "people who are more like her." They never mentioned it to me unless I brought it up. And I had never heard them talk about it to each other before.

It seemed the older I got, the more I thought of them as two really nice white people who'd probably made a big mistake. I wanted to go upstairs and tell them, "Maybe you could find some black family that wouldn't mind taking a kid who isn't a cute, helpless baby. You could tell them the good part is, I won't wet the bed and I have decent manners and it won't be that long before I'll be an adult and they won't have to worry about me anymore."

Meanwhile my mother was up there explaining to my father, "I'm trying to tell you how she feels. Because if I didn't, you wouldn't know. While you are out there in the world doing whatever it is you're doing, I'm here trying to figure out what's best for Lahni."

"Oh, don't start that crap again, Ursula—" Somebody slammed something and I jumped.

"All right. Just know this." My mother's voice was as sharp as a needle going through my skin. "I won't go through this endlessly, for you or for anyone. Either this is your home, or it isn't. Either we're your family, or we're not. When you decide, you let me know. But you won't waltz in here whenever you feel like it and try to make me feel like a piece of crap for trying to be a good mother. I won't stand for it. There's not a chance I will."

My father came out of their bedroom, went into his study, and got his suitcase. He looked at me and shrugged. "I'm sorry, baby," he said quietly. He walked to the front door. "See ya later, pumpkin."

I went upstairs to my room and watched from the window until a taxi came. I was pretty sure he wasn't leaving for good then. But I didn't know how much time my mother and I had. She was strong and so was I. I knew we wouldn't shrivel and die.

I think it was that even though we'd been a weird family, I'd always *tried* to think of us as a family. If my father left, it would feel more like a woman and her adopted daughter. The kid she and her husband had thought they wanted but she got stuck with after the husband left. I wondered how soon it would be before it was obvious to her that the whole thing had been an awful, stinking mistake.

CHAPTER FIVE

"Now, as you know,'" Mr. Faringhelli, our music teacher, read from a typed piece of paper, "'all of the other middle school awards are based on scholarship. However, the arts and athletic awards are different. For these, the students are nominated by their peers.'" Mr. Faringhelli looked up from the paper at us. "And what do I mean by that—'students are nominated by their peers'?"

"You mean that any student trying to get on another student's good side can nominate her," Donna said, looking superior.

"I suppose you could look at it that way." Mr. Faringhelli smiled. "But if that's what the student is up to, she might also consider whether the person has any talent, or else the whole thing backfires and everybody could be embarrassed. Right?"

Donna shrugged. "I guess." Even if one of the girls wanted to get on Donna's good side, it would have been a huge mistake to nominate her for a music award. It wasn't exactly a secret that she was tone deaf. When she sang, she sounded the same as when she was speaking. It was all one low-pitched, sarcastic snarl.

"Remember"—Mr. Faringhelli put the paper down on top of the piano—"if there is more than one nomination, it unfortunately becomes a competition. That means each nominee sings for a jury of judges and a winner is selected. If you are nominated and you really don't feel comfortable with the idea of participating in the competition, you're free to decline the nomination." He waited for a moment, looking around the room. The other girls also were glancing around, trying to figure out who they should nominate. Or maybe just who might nominate *them*.

Mr. Faringhelli picked up his stapler from his desk and tapped it on the top of the piano, grinning. "The floor is now open for nominations for the music department's Best Vocalist Award."

No sooner had he gotten it out of his mouth than Katie's hand shot up. "I nominate Lahni!"

"I decline," I said immediately.

But when I said it, Mr. Faringhelli asked, "Why, Lahni? You have a very sweet voice. I absolutely second the nomination."

I couldn't think fast enough, and I knew if I couldn't come up with a reason right then and there, it would mean I was stuck with the nomination. Part of me was pleased to be nominated, and I felt even better that Mr. Faringhelli had seconded it. But I could also feel, from the looks of the girls around me, that it would mean more weird energy than I could deal with right now.

"No," I said, "I don't think so."

"Well, we'll talk about it, Lahni"—Mr. Faringhelli shook his head— "but I will guarantee, I'm as stubborn as you are. Modesty will get you nowhere." The girls tittered around me, and I knew it definitely wasn't the last time I'd hear that line.

"Is there anyone else you'd like to nominate?"

"Of course. Miss Broadway herself—Amber." Donna was snickering and looking back at Amber. With the two of them, you could never tell exactly what the real story was. Certainly if anybody wanted to be in that competition, Amber Merrill did. So what was the joke—that it was ridiculous to think anybody should get the award but her? I remembered what my mother had said about me thinking they were my enemies all the time. I tried to tell myself Donna's snicker had nothing to do with me, so what did it matter?

About six girls called out their seconding of Amber's nomination. Again I tried not to take Mr. Faringhelli being the only one to second mine personally. I told myself it was just a coincidence.

"I nominate Lisa Shin." Katie was really on a roll. It was true Lisa Shin had a pretty voice, but why had Katie suddenly appointed herself a one-person nominating committee?

There was a really awkward moment of silence. So none of the little witches could bring themselves to second anyone else's nomination but Amber's? I'd have done it, but I was too busy concentrating on how to get out of my own. Mr. Faringhelli wasn't taking any chances. Before any more time went by, he clapped his hands and said, "Another great nomination, Katie! I'll use my executive privilege and second that one, too!"

I looked over at Katie, who had the widest grin I'd seen on her in a while. Mr. Faringhelli asked, "Do we have any more?" I'm sure there were girls who wanted to hear their names called, but it didn't happen. No one wanted to make a fool of themselves by competing with Amber. Like Donna said, she was "Miss Broadway." According to her, she'd seen about a hundred and sixty shows and knew the songs from most of them. Even if she didn't have the greatest voice in the world, it was definitely the loudest, and everyone assumed it was one we'd all be hearing long after we graduated from Darby.

Finally Mr. Faringhelli said, "Well, okay then. We have three nominees, which automatically makes them finalists in the competition. I'll work with the nominees on song choice, and the dean will ask three judges from outside the school to choose the winner for this year's middle school talent competition."

Katie looked over at me, still grinning. I'm sure she didn't think I'd actually go to Mr. Faringhelli and get out of it, but that was exactly what I was planning to do. And as soon as I possibly could.

After class most of the girls gathered around Amber as though she were the only one in the competition. Amber was already performing. "I can't wait for the coaching sessions. I'm going to tell him I'll sing anything he wants me to sing," she said. Then she ran her hands down her body, trying to look sexy. "Wearing whatever he wants me to wear while I'm singing it." There were lots of oohs and aahs as though it were the cleverest thing anyone had heard in years.

Donna, of course, had to add her two and a half cents. "If he's too chicken to do anything with you in his classroom, tell him it's so late, he'll have to give you a ride home. If you can't get anything going with him in his car, call me and I'll give you some big-girl tips." The girls oohed again and giggled.

Amber turned in my direction. "I really think Lahni is Mr. Faringhelli's favorite." She pretended to pout. "He even said, right there in front of all of us, 'Modesty, Lahni, will get you nowhere.'" The girls waited for my reaction. I shrugged and faked a smile. Then I started down the hall with Katie following me.

I wasn't blind; I saw what the other girls saw. Mr. Faringhelli probably wasn't thirty yet, which made him the youngest Darby faculty member by far. He looked tanned all year round and had gray eyes and shiny black hair that kept falling over his forehead when he spoke. He was also single, and no one thought he might be gay, like they did Mr. Jameson, the history teacher, or Mr. Cabriette, the French teacher. There was always just the slightest smell of coffee on Mr. Faringhelli's breath, and we could see him from our English room's window, drinking it from a paper cup and smoking little butts of cigarettes in the parking lot between classes. Most of the time, one of the few things that we all agreed on was that cigarettes and coffee breath were both a disaster, but on Mr. Faringhelli, somehow the combination was considered pretty hot.

He wore white shirts that looked like he sent them out to be starched, but after about fifteen minutes in class, he pulled at his tie and unbuttoned his top button. His underarms got darker and darker, and when he rolled up his sleeves, his forearms were sweaty. When his shirt was even more damp, you could see the outline of his chest and his nipples stuck out.

"Did you see them today?" Amber would ask when we were barely out of class, and everyone knew what she meant.

"Nicky's nipples are as big as mine," Donna once said, and we all laughed, even me. You could always count on Donna to say stuff nobody else would dare to, especially about body parts and sex. Donna was the first one to start calling Mr. Faringhelli "Nicky" behind his back.

When we had music class, either Mr. Faringhelli ran in late, smelling of cigarettes, or he'd be sitting at the piano playing jazz with his head bobbing and his eyes closed. His hair would be flopping up and down, and I'd be embarrassed at the look on his face.

He'd open his eyes and laugh. "How y'all doin' today?" The other girls would giggle. "Ya caught me," he'd say, pushing away from the piano, and they'd giggle again. "Today, you're gonna sing like you've never sung before." He'd point to us, and the whole room would slump in their seats and there'd be another *tee-hee-hee*.

• • •

For the rest of the afternoon, I got teased with "Modesty will get you nowhere." I kept thinking about how I would soon go back to Mr. Faringhelli and tell him in private there was no way I was going to compete. I didn't consider myself a real singer, not like the ones I admired. Sure, I daydreamed about standing on a stage and having people get goose bumps when I sang, but doesn't everybody? Katie and I had a saying we got from Mr. Jameson, the history teacher. "Do not confuse myth with reality." Once he said it in class, we stole it whenever we heard one of our classmates lying about something. We'd mumble under our breath, "Do not, girls, confuse myth with reality." That's how I felt about my singing. On a good day, I thought my voice was fine. But I never let myself get carried away with the Lahni-becomes-a-superstar daydream. Not for a second. Besides, I didn't want to be in a competition for anything, especially against Amber Merrill. It was like calling attention to yourself and saying, "Watch me lose."

The strange thing was, it was still exciting to be nominated. I couldn't wait to get home to tell Mom. Even though I knew it wouldn't be that much fun having her try to convince me to stay in the competition.

As we rode our bikes home, Katie yelled over to me, "Don't you think it's great?"

"I would if I thought it made sense." I wasn't sure

of everything I thought about it, but I wasn't going to take the chance of thinking any of it out loud to Katie. With what was going on between my mother and father, my new motto was, "Trust no one. They all change their minds eventually."

I knew from the minute I saw her standing there in the living room, looking as though she'd been waiting hours for me, Mom had her own news.

I barely got a "hi" out before she said, "Lahni, honey, come into the kitchen."

I followed her. There was a plate of mint-chocolate Girl Scout cookies and a copy of the *New Clarion Advocate* spread out on the kitchen table. "Sit down," Mom said. "I want to talk to you about something."

I sat and laughed, pointing to the plate of cookies. "You haven't been sitting here eating these by yourself, have you?" Mom—Miss Two-Mile Run Before Breakfast—shook her head indignantly, as though I'd asked her if she'd been hiding doughnuts and ice cream in her closet.

"No, honey, they're for you. And I want you to take a look at this and tell me what you think."

She sat across from me and pushed the paper toward me. It was the page where all the churches in the city were advertised. One of them, an ad for Church of the Good

Shepherd, had a green Magic Marker circle around it.

I didn't understand. We didn't go to church. We'd never gone to church. We didn't pray, we didn't talk about God. I personally thought there was one, but I wasn't even sure how I'd come to that conclusion. And it definitely hadn't been with the help of my parents. I just thought there was something comforting about someone else making sure things worked out all right in the end.

The ad that was circled for Church of the Good Shepherd said, "Interdenominational. We welcome all—regardless of race, creed, or sexual orientation."

"Mom, I don't get it. What is the point?"

"The point is I think we should go check it out."

"Check it out? Why? Mom, this is crazy. Why now?"

"Why not now? I don't know about you, but I could use some church right about now. Besides, it's probably a place where you can meet some . . . other types of kids." She meant black kids, I was sure. This was what she'd come up with after arguing with my dad about me.

She reached for not one, but two cookies and put them in front of her. "When I first met your father in New York, I was going to church every Sunday. But it wasn't something he was interested in, so after a while, I stopped going. The last time I was in a church was the day we got married."

"So you believe in God?"

"Of course I do." She looked at me surprised, as though she couldn't believe I didn't know the answer. What *was* hard for me to believe was if going to church had been important to her at all, why had she stopped going because of my father?

"Well, if you want to go back, I guess I'll go with you." I bit into a cookie and looked at the ad again. "But we don't have to go just because you think there'll be some black kids there for me to meet."

Mom was already on her second mint-chocolate sandwich. "Honey, it's as much for me as it is for you. Believe me." When I looked across the table at her, I saw how swollen and red her eyes looked. Suddenly it occurred to me that maybe she was having a nervous breakdown because of what was going on with my father. If she *was*, maybe this church thing was a way of trying to help herself. Either way, I thought, we have nothing to lose.

CHAPTER SIX

"Well, we made it," Mom said as we parked on the side of Elizabeth Road.

"Barely," I answered.

The newspaper had said, "Service begins promptly at 11:00 a.m." Mom called the church for directions to Elizabeth Road. We'd both raced out of the house at 10:40.

Now Mom was checking her teeth in the mirror for lipstick. Then she looked at me, as if for one final agreement that we were going to do this.

"C'mon," I told her. "We practically killed ourselves getting here; I don't want to walk in late." I jumped out of the car and started down the road.

Church of the Good Shepherd was closer to the suburbs of New Clarion, where we lived. It was at the dead end of a winding road with a big, raggedy looking field behind it. Cars were parked on both sides of the road, so I was pretty sure there would be more people than me, Mom, and the minister inside. I wasn't sure how many or what they'd be like, though.

The church itself was low and long, like a lot of churches in the New Clarion suburbs. It was a dark-red brick building. A thin, silver-colored cross looked like it was growing out of the back of it. At the end of the walkway leading up to the church was a sign that said CHURCH OF THE GOOD SHEPHERD. LET THE SPIRIT OF HOPE THAT LED YOU HERE BE WITH YOU ALWAYS. I looked at my mother. She'd put on her dark glasses, so I couldn't see her eyes. A few gray strands of her dyed-once-a-month brown hair glistened in the sun. She wore a black linen dress and heels. It didn't take much to make her look dressed up, I thought. My father didn't seem to agree with me. Whenever they were going out together, he would wait until they were ready to leave and say to her, "I thought you told me you were getting dressed for this."

I had on a skirt that was a little too big, so I'd worn a belt to keep it from sliding down, and a blouse over the skirt so you couldn't see how bunched up the belt was. My mother was elegant. One of the crummy things about being adopted, I thought, was that the good stuff, like being elegant, you could never inherit. I could learn by watching my mother, but it would never be in "my blood." And for her I guess my being adopted was good because no one could ever blame her for my bad taste. She could just say that it came with me. Not that I thought she would.

There was a sweet-looking, older white couple on either side of the church entrance. They handed us programs and said, "Welcome, welcome, so happy to have you," like CD speakers playing the same song but at different speeds.

Mom and I started down the center aisle. It wasn't a very wide church, but it was a long way to the front. I thought Mom might be nervous, because she was walking so fast and going so far down the aisle.

"Mom, stop," I whispered. "Mom!" She stopped at about the seventh row from the front and turned to me. "Is this too far, honey?"

I just shrugged and squeezed past several people who were already sitting.

Once we sat, I realized how pretty the church was. It had stained glass windows that were mostly shades of red, blue, and purple. I hadn't seen a lot of stained glass. The more I looked around, the more I could pick out shapes and faces in the windows. Hands, birds, fish. No Jesus that I could see. But I was pretty sure he had to be in there somewhere.

It was true, like the ad said, there were different kinds of people there—a few Asians, old people, several black families, some younger couples with whiny babies. They were mostly white, though. I guess I'd imagined that every other person in each row would look like they'd come from another country. There weren't any black kids my age that I could see. I wasn't exactly disappointed—I was never all that excited about trying to make friends—but I did have to admit I'd been curious to see if there were any black kids at Good Shepherd.

I looked at Mom. She still had her dark glasses on. It was a neat trick, I thought, how dark glasses could act as a wall between you and the world. Who could tell what she was thinking? And yet she had a great view of the whole works.

The kettle-shaped man playing the organ was black, but he and my mother had something in common. He also was wearing dark glasses. Maybe he's blind, I thought. If not, he's pretty rude being the church organist and wearing dark glasses in front of everyone while he's playing. True, there was a pale, purplish light shining on him from the stained glass window above the organ, but there definitely wasn't enough glare to require dark glasses.

To be honest, I also thought the fact that he was black was pretty startling. I checked my program and read that he was playing a Bach prelude. I'd never seen a black man playing an organ live before, much less playing Bach. All the black men I'd seen in movies playing church organs were usually jumping, shouting, and practically dancing up and down the organ keys. There'd been a few organ concerts at Darby with white organists playing Bach, but it never occurred to me that I'd ever see or hear a black organist playing that kind of music. But then, I thought, looking over at my mother's pale knees peeking out from under her skirt, I hadn't seen black people do much of anything live before.

I looked at the organist's name in the program. Marcus Delacroix III. If he wasn't famous already, I was sure he would be soon. Maybe that explained the dark glasses. Maybe he was cocky because he was so talented. It sounded to me like he had twenty-five fingers on each hand. The notes went up and down like raindrops in a thunderstorm. When he finished, I wanted to clap, but I figured I wasn't supposed to. He started right in on a different song, anyway, and everyone stood and opened their hymnals. The song was one we'd learned in lower school, "Glory, Glory, Hallelujah." It was about laying your burdens down and feeling so much better.

Mom still hadn't taken off her own dark glasses, so I didn't think she was going to sing. I began quietly singing the soprano descant that Miss Gleason, the lower-school music teacher, had taught us.

In the aisle, the choir was passing us on its way to the front of the church. They had on navy blue robes with wide, shiny, red satin stoles. The only thing that made each choir member look different was how short or tall they were, their heads and faces, and their shoes. I don't know why, but as the members stepped up to the altar, I started wondering what they had on under their robes. What if somebody was wearing one over just underwear with nice shoes? Who would ever know?

I was pretty excited to hear the combination of women's voices—they were in the front—and then the men's. But what was even more exciting was that there were more black people in the choir than in the rest of the church. If nothing else, Mom and I would probably hear some good singing. The trip to Good Shepherd would be worth it, if just for that.

Most of the choir members seemed to know the "Glory, Glory, Hallelujah" song by heart also, so they just marched and clapped without looking at the words. Some of the other people in the pews were clapping too, which I hadn't expected. I wasn't sure I could do both at the same time, so I concentrated on singing the descant.

But the next thing I heard was Mom. "I am dancing

Mary's dance now, since I laid my burdens down." Not only was she singing, she was clapping, too, and swaying to the music.

I thought, *Yep. This is it. She's having a nervous breakdown because of my butthead father. She'll probably start crying and make a huge scene, and we'll have to leave.* I looked up at her. She still had her dark glasses on, rocking back and forth, singing louder and louder. *I wonder if there's a doctor in here. Maybe if it gets really bad, he'll see her and help us.* I decided I wasn't going to be embarrassed, no matter what Mom did. I just wanted her to be all right. *You're a real creep to do this to her, Timothy Schuler. Wherever you are.*

The song must have had seventeen verses, but when we finished it, Mom sat down, put her arm around me, and squeezed my shoulders. She leaned down and asked, "Isn't this great?"

I turned to her. "Are you all right?"

"Of course, baby. Are you?"

"Yeah. Sure. I'm fine."

I figured the worst was over for a while. Maybe the breakdown wasn't going to happen just yet. Or if we were lucky, not at all. Maybe Mom just felt good in church, like she said. But I still could have killed my father. He wasn't here, and Mom was already doing things she'd never done as long as I'd known her.

The minister stood up at that point. I hadn't even noticed him coming in, because I was so preoccupied with Mom. He was white, and about fifty, I thought, and so thin his robe made him look like Ichabod Crane from "The Legend of Sleepy Hollow." He had little wire-rimmed glasses that he wiped a few times before he spoke. "Welcome," he said, "to anyone who has never joined us here before at Church of the Good Shepherd." He must've known for sure that Mom and I were strangers, because he looked right at us when he said it. He invited all the newcomers for coffee after the service. I didn't think we'd go, but I wondered if they served anything special for kids who were new. I wasn't all that fond of coffee.

The minister prayed a very long prayer for peace in the country, abroad, and in New Clarion. He practically repeated the whole "Glory, Glory" song, especially the part about laying your burdens down. He named about ten different burdens people could have, from alcoholism to mourning the death of someone close to you, and people called out, "Amen!"—I guess for the ones they could especially relate to.

When he finished, the organ played just enough for the choir to sing about six more "amens" in a round—sopranos, then tenors and baritones, and finally basses.

The minister, Reverend Fred Caffrey, said, "I encourage

you now to pass the peace among your neighbors." I hadn't any idea what he was talking about. But the church members left their pews and went around the church shaking hands and saying, "Peace be with you," to one another. It wasn't exactly hard to remember so Mom and I did it, too. She was a lot friendlier than I was. I said it to a few people, very quietly, but I never left the pew. A very pink woman with a high pile of orange-yellow hair and a snug dress with giant dandelions painted on it cut through a few people to get to my mother. I knew from the dandelions, her perfume, and the way she'd pushed through the others that she was bad news.

"Are you two together?" she asked my mom. No "hello." No "peace be with you." Just a phony smile and the stupid question. What she really seemed to be asking was, *So what's the story here?* Her smile could have cracked the stained glass windows.

"Yes, we are together," my mother said cheerily. "I'm Ursula Schuler and this is my daughter, Lahni." She put her arm around me again.

"And do you all live in this area?" the big, pink dandelion asked.

"Yes, we do," my mother said, still using her voice that sounded like a bird chirping.

"Well, isn't that nice," the dandelion said. She stepped

back and took another look at me. "You're a big girl, aren't you?"

I pretended I hadn't heard a word. "Peace to you," I said, and smiled a smile I usually used on Donna and Amber when I wanted them to go away quickly.

By this time most people were back in their seats. The minister came forward and chuckled. "We people of Good Shepherd love to pass the peace, don't we?" The church laughed.

The dandelion looked as though she'd run out of time before she got all the information she wanted. She stopped smiling like someone had pulled a plug at the back of her dress. Then she turned as suddenly as she'd appeared and went to the back of the church. I could still smell her perfume. Fanning myself with my program, I crinkled my nose and looked up at my mother for her reaction, but there wasn't any.

"Why do you still have on your glasses?" I whispered.

My mother stuck her tongue out at me. "You're a big girl, aren't you?" She'd done a perfect imitation of the pink dandelion. Laughing, she took off her dark glasses. We sat down with our arms against each other's. My mother smelled like bath powder. *She's like a baby today,* I thought. *My baby.*

Reverend Caffrey announced, "The solo of the morning

will now be sung by Carietta Chisolm." I looked at my program to make sure I'd heard correctly. Carietta Chisolm? It sounded like a name from a little kid's book.

Carietta Chisolm was even rounder than Marcus Delacroix III, which was saying a lot. The two of them, him sitting at the organ and her walking up to the microphone, made me think of these salt and pepper shakers we used in the summer for barbecues. Each of them was made of two balls of light brown wood, one sitting on top of another. They were painted to look like chefs, a man and a woman in mushroom-top white hats and jackets. Both of them had big eyes, long eyelashes, and shiny red mouths. The only difference was the man had a mustache. If you put the two of them together, you knew this was a couple that ate everything they cooked. And enjoyed every bit of it. That's what Marcus Delacroix III and Carietta Chisolm looked like at the front of the church. Round, brown, salt and pepper shakers with hair, in navy blue robes with red satin stoles.

Carietta Chisolm wasn't just a plumper, she was probably the most beautiful woman in the room. Besides Ursula Schuler, of course. Even from where we were sitting, I could see she had huge eyelashes, a button nose, and dimples. Her straightened hair was pulled back, and she had the longest ponytail I'd ever seen on anything besides a real pony. And her shoes were as red as her choir stole, except that they had very high heels that were clear. They looked like glass, but, of course, I knew they were probably hard plastic. I'd never in my life seen anyone wearing shoes with clear plastic heels.

Marcus Delacroix III started playing these low notes that would go on forever, then these really quick ones that swooped like birds flying low over our heads. I looked up at Mom. She was smiling with her eyes closed.

Then Carietta Chisolm put her mouth close to the microphone and started singing, "Aaaah." She did the same thing with her "aaaah" that Mr. Delacroix had done with his organ playing. She started really low and soft, then, as easy as maple syrup pouring over pancakes, she went up, up into a voice that shimmered like crystal in sunlight.

I wasn't sure, but I thought I knew what she was singing. "Aaa Maa Ziing, soooo Aaaa Maaa Ziing. Graaaaaace. Howuuuuu Sweeeet, sweet, the so-ou-ound!" I'd heard it a thousand times, but never, never like this. "Thaaaaat saved, do you hear me say saved, a chiiiiillld like me-ee-eeee!" A feeling went through me that mashed me flat as an ironing board against the pew. Before I knew it, both legs kicked right out in front of me. I wanted to jump up and run down the aisle to get closer to Carietta Chisolm. I wanted to stand next to her and Marcus Delacroix III playing the organ and dance the dance of Amazing Grace, how sweet the sound! What was happening to me?

I looked at Mom. She was swaying back and forth in her seat. Tears were running down her cheeks. But she was smiling. Her dark glasses slid off her lap and onto the church carpet. Neither of us moved to pick them up. Carietta Chisolm was singing that she was lost, lost, lost—but now, she knew she'd finally reached her home—that she'd been blind—ever since she could remember—but now—

And that's when she stopped. The organ stopped. I took a deep breath because I thought I was going to faint. I looked up at Carietta Chisolm, wondering what had happened to her so suddenly. She was standing with her head bowed so low, you could see the topknot of her ponytail, the size of a baby's fist. Her arms were outstretched like she was a big, brown and navy blue bird about to take off. You could hear her breathing heavily into the microphone, but nobody looked like they were going to help her. Just as I started to get really worried, Carietta threw her head back and started a scream—"Iiiiiiiiii"—that turned into a note so high it sounded as if she could have opened a seam in the roof with her voice. "I seeeeeee!!!"

Mom was sobbing next to me like a little girl. People around us were shouting "amen" and waving their hands in the air. I kept looking to the front at Carietta Chisolm. She was doing a little dance in her red shoes with the plastic heels, shaking her ponytail from side to side, and fanning herself with her long, long red nails. She was truly beautiful. They should make a doll, I decided. A Carietta Chisolm Gospel Singer Doll. In a navy blue robe, with red shoes and plastic heels. A ponytail to her waist and long red nails. But they could never in a million years get a doll to sing like that. Even with a recorded voice inside her, it wouldn't be like hearing the real thing.

If I could be Carietta Chisolm, I thought, for only one day, I swear I would open my mouth and just keep singing. What else would I need? What else could I possibly need?

CHAPTER SEVEN

Monday morning I saw the weird guy again. Red High-tops. Katie and I had agreed we'd ride our bikes to school together. We met at the corner of Sycamore and Vernon Roads and headed toward Darby. All the roads in our area were woodsy and quiet, like a never-ending forest. No horns, no voices.

The Darby School and The Kent Academy are both set back off the road like the houses are. There's a rule that bikes can go only single file on the road that leads to Darby's main entrance. When we turned off Sycamore, Katie dropped to the back. I took the lead.

That's when I heard hip-hop blaring behind me, the bass thumping like early morning thunder cutting through the stillness. The thumping got closer. Then it was right beside me. A white Toyota, I think. I glanced over because I thought it would pass me, but it didn't. The noise was ugly, obnoxious.

Slowly the car was moving alongside me. When I looked over, I saw Red High-tops. He was staring at me the same way he had on the athletic field. Like he was about to say something. He had his window down so it seemed as though he could reach out if he wanted to and touch me. He turned the music down. Then he leaned toward me. It looked like he was about to smile. Instead, he made this clicking sound with his teeth. Like a cricket. Quick, loud, clicking. I looked away quickly and pedaled faster.

He sped up. I watched him make a U-turn at Darby's front entrance, which is illegal; then he was coming toward me again, with the hip-hop still thumping. "Gonna get ya high, uh-huh, uh-huh. Gonna make ya holla, uh-huh, uh-huh. The way you make me feeeall, yeah, got to keep it reaall, yeah." When he drove past me again, I huddled over my handlebars, afraid for him to get near me. The softer his music got, the farther away I knew he was from me.

We were at the main entrance. I jumped off my bike and walked it around the side to the racks. Katie caught up with me. "What was that guy's problem?"

"I have no idea." I eased my front wheel into the rack, hoping she would drop the subject.

"Do you know him?"

I turned to Katie. "It was that guy who Donna said asked about me."

"Ohmygodohmygodohmygod! That was him?" Katie shrieked. "The same guy we saw running, in the red Keds? Holy crap! Did you see how he was driving?"

"Did I have a choice?" I asked her.

That afternoon, I decided to tell Mr. Faringhelli once and for all I wasn't singing in the competition, even if he did think my voice was—what did he call it?—"sweet." Well, "sweet" wasn't going to win any prizes, and I wasn't in the mood to have anybody make a fool of me.

I went to his classroom after school, ready with my speech. Mr. Faringhelli gave me this huge smile when I walked in and said, "Just the person I want to see." He went to the piano. "Do you know this?" He was barely on the bench when he started playing and singing.

> "Where is the sun
> in a sky of gray?
> Can you find home
> when you've gone astray?"

"No, I don't," I answered quietly. I thought, *I bet he'd rather be a performer than a teacher.* He leaned back and put his head up toward the ceiling, with his eyes half closed, then fell forward over the piano, very low, with his shoulders hunched. There was the half smile on his face that made me a little embarrassed, although I wasn't sure why exactly. But I couldn't stop watching him. Mostly, I think, because whenever he sang, he was telling a story. And he was enjoying telling the story so much, you couldn't help but watch him, even if it did make you feel like maybe he was telling something too personal for you to hear. It had been the same way when Carietta Chisolm sang on Sunday. Even though her eyes were closed, I still knew she was telling her story for her, but also for everyone else, with all of those sounds that rumbled, then flew.

Mr. Faringhelli finished his song with a long high note, leaning back singing the question, "When will I know that I'm hoooome?" For a second I thought of how jealous Donna and the other girls would be, seeing me alone with him. I smiled. Mr. Faringhelli caught me. "So you like that, huh?"

"Um . . . you mean the song?"

"Of course, the song. I wouldn't dare ask about the singing. I'm not the singer. You are."

I shook my head and put up my hand to tell him to stop. "Mr. Faringhelli, I am not a singer, and I'm absolutely not competition material."

He stood up from the piano and sighed loudly. "Why is it every student, including me back when I was one, thinks all teachers couldn't possibly know even half of what they know?"

"Mr. Faringhelli, I think you're a really good teacher. I just—"

"You think even though I have three degrees in music and have led umpteen choral groups, it's not possible I'd be able to pick out a voice with considerable potential if I heard one?"

"I think you're trying to be nice to me—"

"And why would I want to do that? You're already a good student, Lahni. It's not as though you aren't doing well in my class, anyway. Why would I decide you needed an act of charity? And why would I risk sponsoring you as your teacher so that I looked ridiculous too?"

I looked at the floor, frowning. Obviously, I hadn't thought my argument out well enough.

Mr. Faringhelli sat back down at the piano, staring at the sheet music in front of him. "If you don't like the song, it's not a problem. I just thought it would be good for you because it shows the range of your voice. Also Lahni, you tend to be a bit conservative when you sing. This song has a lot of feeling. I thought it might open you up a bit."

Conservative? Open me up a bit? I was shocked. And even if I didn't really know anything about singing, I did know just from the sound of it, "conservative" was not the kind of singer I wanted to be.

"Yes," I agreed quietly. "That song does have a lot of feeling. I like it. It's fine."

"Well, it should be *your* choice. You can't get excited about performing if you don't love the material. Do you want to try it?"

"Sure." I stood as straight as I could, stuck my chest out and held my breath.

"Relax," Mr. Faringhelli said in a low, husky voice. "Breathe."

He began to play, bobbing back and forth to his own accompaniment. I wasn't sure where to come in. When I realized he'd started over, I knew I'd missed my cue. This time, when he got to where I should start, he nodded to me and sang himself, very softly. I began with him, and a few words later he stopped singing, leaving me on my own.

We went through to the end without any mistakes. I figured that was because his playing was so good. It was as though he kept sending out waves, and I could make the decision to float or really stroke and kick, except using only my voice to get from one place to the other. When he turned the last page of music and we finished together, I got a slight chill. I knew something good had happened between us. Even if how I sang didn't have that much to do with it.

"Well, what do you think?"

What did I think? It seemed to me that competitions were dumb. The only reasons to enter a competition were so (1) you could show off, (2) your parents could be proud of you, and (3) they would have something to brag about. At that moment I wasn't at all interested in showing off; my parents couldn't be bothered with whether I could sing or tap dance or balance beach balls on my nose while I was doing both. So what was the point?

"Mr. Faringhelli, I appreciate your confidence in me. I really do. But I'd still just as soon not compete. Will that be a problem?" *In other words, will you flunk me if I don't?*

Mr. Faringhelli sat back on the piano stool and folded his hands in his lap, looking down at them. He had what my mom called "cow lashes." I looked from them down to his nose and mouth. There was a shadow of a mustache above his upper lip, and below it, a short, wide chin with a deep cleft in it. When I was younger, I asked my mother how cleft chins happened. I'd thought it was sad that people were born with bits of their chins missing. She'd laughed and explained that it wasn't a defect at all, it was simply another thing that made people different. Mr.

Faringhelli was the first person I actually knew with a cleft, and all the girls thought it made him extra cute. Personally, I wanted to ask him if it ever made him feel freakish, if he'd rather have a chin without a big dent in it.

A few inches down on his throat, was a rough red line, a scratch where maybe he'd cut himself shaving. Below that, where his shirt collar was open, were tiny black curls of hair.

I thought back to the conversation with the girls about Mr. Faringhelli "trying something" with me. My guess was that he probably had a girlfriend. They had lots of sex every night and four times a day on the weekends. Why on earth would he want a skinny eighth grader with hardly any breasts and a flat butt?

Mr. Faringhelli swung his legs over the piano bench so that he was straddling it like a horse. He leaned toward me. It wasn't that close, but still it somehow made me feel like stepping back.

"No. It's not a problem for me if you remove yourself from the competition." He shrugged. "But . . . I think it may be a problem for you."

See. Just what I was afraid of. He is going to blackmail me by telling me either I sing in the competition or he'll give me a crummy grade.

"The problem for you, Lahni, is that you'd rather say

no to the possibility of being recognized for your talent than put the best that you have out there and see what happens. Yes, I do think that's a problem. And I'm sorry to see it in someone as young as you are."

I looked at the walls, the floor, the ceiling, the top of the piano—anywhere but at Mr. Faringhelli.

"Mr. Faringhelli, I love to sing. I sing all the time. Riding my bike. In the grocery store. I make up songs and write down the words so I won't forget them. But I've never thought my voice was anything special. I keep thinking you must be hearing someone else and thinking it's me."

"But I heard you just now, didn't I? Lahni, I'm not saying it won't take work and rehearsal. But I wouldn't be here wasting my time if I didn't think you had some promise."

"Promise"? What a strange word to use. Did that mean I could either keep my "promise" or break it?

I stood there staring at his shoes now. Usually, in a situation like this, I would think of my dad. What would he say? What would he want me to do? Should I stall and say I want to think it over and then run home to call him and talk about it? I knew this time it was impossible.

I thought about all the times we had sung together in the car, going back and forth to the store, figuring out harmonies, laughing at each other when one of us was singing off-key. *But when was the last time the two of you sang together in the car, Lahni? Or anywhere, for that matter? Can you think that far back? How about a good dose of reality?*

"Mr. Faringhelli, are you coaching Lisa and Amber?"

"Well, I'm trying to be fair to all three of you. So I'm suggesting songs and offering some very general coaching—just to help you get your voices in shape. I've offered to work with Lisa and Amber for a couple of hours each week up until the competition."

"Do you think you could fit me in?"

"I'm positive of it. Have you talked about the competition with your parents?"

"Yes. Sure. They really want me to do it. I was the one who was . . . undecided." I grabbed my backpack and slung it over my shoulder. Having just told a whopping big lie, I was anxious to get out of there.

Mr. Faringhelli said, "Look over your schedule and tell me what the best days are for you."

"Thank you. I will." I was already backing toward the door.

"Oh, and Lahni—here. I made a tape for you to work with. It has 'When Will I Know When I'm Home?' on it, in case you decide that's definitely what you want to perform."

I grabbed the tape. "Thank you, Mr. Faringhelli. Thanks a lot. I'll do my best." And I was out of there. All the way down the hall, I could still see his outstretched hand with the tape in it, and the big smile on his face. I couldn't believe this competition thing meant that much to him. Funny, I was deciding right at that moment not to say anything about it to either of my parents, and Mr. Faringhelli had talked to me like if I did compete, *he'd* be proud of me. I had thought maybe I could get away with doing the whole thing and not have anybody care one way or the other. But it didn't look like that was going to happen. *Dear Nicky Faringhelli. Thanks a lot for sucking me in just like all the other girls at Darby. Thanks a lot.*

Wednesday morning most of the eighth grade was standing in front of the bulletin board in the music and art department. It didn't matter if we didn't go into class immediately. Mr. Faringhelli wasn't exactly a stickler on punctuality. When we saw him barreling down the hallway trying not to spill his paper cup of coffee, that's when we rushed into class to be there ahead of him—seconds ahead of him.

The announcement on the bulletin board said MUSIC DEPARTMENT'S BEST VOCALIST COMPETITION FINALISTS. I felt a little light-headed when I saw how formal it looked. Of course,

I'd seen lots of lists posted on bulletin boards all over the building. Some of them had had my name on them, along with everyone else's in my class. But I'd never been on a list at Darby with just two other people and never one that anyone else wanted to be on and wasn't. I was reading the other two names for the first time myself when Donna came up behind me and read them out loud. "Lahni Schuler, Lisa Shin, Amber Merrill. Well, you go Nicky boy! Nicky Faringhelli and his United Nations Talent Competition. One black girl, one Korean girl, and one all-American white girl! You should run for president, Nicky."

Katie squeezed my arm. The other girls snickered half-heartedly but loud enough so that I think I was the only one who heard Katie whisper "creep!" under her breath.

Amber said to Donna, "You are soooo jealous, Donna, you can't stand it." Then she turned and went into class. It was wonderful. Even though Amber was by far not my favorite girl in the eighth grade, I had to give her credit for telling the truth for once.

I just kept pretending to be reading the other announcements on the board. No one else who was standing there mentioned anything about the Drama Club nominating Anne Seacrest for the talent competition too. The pack didn't seem to think Anne Seacrest was important enough to be concerned about, one way or another.

When Mr. Faringhelli came, some of the girls like Donna and Cyndi didn't even bother trying to beat him into the classroom. They chatted with each other until he got right up to the door and asked them, "Well? Are we having class today or aren't we?" On some other day, there would have been giggling. But not today. Nobody answered. They just slouched in as though they'd go in all right, but they'd take their sweet time getting in there.

Finally Mr. Faringhelli said, "Is something going on here that I should know about?"

Again no one answered. Mr. Faringhelli took out his roll book for our class and started reading from the top. About halfway through the names, he stopped for a moment and took a long look at the class as if he was confused. Then he continued but in a different tone of voice. When he finished, he put the roll book down, came around to the front of his desk, and sat on the edge of it. His tie was hanging down around his collarbone, his shirt unbuttoned behind the tie. He rerolled one of his sleeves up. His tan arms were shiny with perspiration.

"Before we do anything today, I want to talk about this end of the year talent competition." Out of the corner of my eye, I saw Donna drop her head back and sink into her seat like she was already bored beyond belief. She looked up at the ceiling as though Mr. Faringhelli had said, "I want to tell you about the origin of the housefly and how it pertains to the history of the American West." I licked my lips and tried to look calm and attentive in case anybody was looking at me.

"I think we should congratulate Lisa, Amber, and Lahni and tell them we wish all of them good luck. After all, you nominated them, so I'm hoping you will support them. Some of you will be nominated in the other categories, athletics and scholarship. It's hard at the end of the year because of all the pressure to do well, and to be up for these prizes can be nerve-racking too. All of you have some special talent, and eventually, hopefully that talent will receive recognition. If it doesn't happen this June, don't worry about it. The point is not to get a medal or plaque with your name engraved on it. The point is to work hard at what you do, and there's no way people won't notice that, because they will. You just gotta keep at it. Make sense?"

He sounded like a coach giving a speech to a team in the movies. If he was trying to get some people to accept that they weren't nominated, I knew it wasn't working. I don't even believe he thought it worked. He wiped his shiny forehead with his sleeve.

"And don't forget," he said, looking at me, Lisa, and Amber as though he didn't really want to keep talking about it, "if I haven't already talked to you about this, you should make a coaching appointment with me sooner rather than later. We have about four weeks before the competition." I was just grateful he hadn't mentioned our conversation.

When none of us answered, he stood up and looked at each of us hard. "You hearing me, ladeez?"

"Yes, Mr. Faringhelli," the three of us said not quite in unison.

Mr. Faringhelli grinned back at us and gave us a thumbs-up. Let them be jealous, I decided. What difference does it make? I'm going to try for this thing anyway. No matter what anybody thinks.

CHAPTER EIGHT

The war behind my parents' bedroom door was longer and louder than it had ever been. That Friday night the last thing I thought my father would be interested in hearing about was a silly competition. Especially one I couldn't believe I got into in the first place. Even though I'd waited all week to tell him, I spent most of Friday night eavesdropping so I'd know the truth about how bad things were between my mother and him.

"I actually found myself waiting for you to get here tonight, Tim." That's how my mom started. "I was looking forward to it so I could ask you how long you think you can keep this up."

Silence.

Then, "Urs, why do you do this? Why do you make yourself suffer like this? Why can't we just get through one weekend without you having a tantrum and upsetting everything?"

"I just want you to make up your mind what it is you want to do. You come back here when you feel like it, and you want us all to play house until you go away again for God knows how long. I don't want to do it anymore."

"Urs—"

"Does she know you have a family?"

I froze. Who was "she"? Was there really a "she"?

"Ursula, don't!"

"No! For once, make up your mind about something. It's always this way with you. Always! You can't make a decision. Now is no different. Except now you're not just playing with my life, you're playing with Lahni's. And that is making me angrier than anything. Do what you're going to do, Tim, whatever it is. And Lahni and I will be fine, come what may!"

Back in January, I'd asked him why he traveled more often and stayed away longer. "We're opening all these new offices throughout Germany and Belgium, honey. I'm the only one who can get them started the way they should be. If I'm not there and something goes wrong, it's *my* head on the block." He was watching my eyes for my reaction. "Believe me, it's frustrating for me, too. I'll be glad when it's over."

He'd paced around the kitchen with both hands in his pockets, looking lost between the stove and the refrigerator. He stopped in the middle of the room under the light, and I stared at his gray curls. They'd been gray ever since I could remember. He had said that they'd starting turning gray before he was twenty.

"When *will* it be over?" I'd asked him. What I was asking about was his traveling, but I felt like I was asking something even scarier. I remember watching *his* eyes just as he'd watched mine.

Be careful. Don't think I won't know if you're telling the truth or not, because I will.

My father had turned to me with his hands still in his pockets. "I don't know, hon. I really don't."

That Friday night in April, when he caught me eavesdropping on the stairs, I wanted to ask him again if he knew how long what was happening to us would go on. How close were we to the end? But I didn't ask him anything. He asked me. He looked surprised to see me at first, standing there on the staircase. Then he took one of my ears and squeezed it. "You okay?" he asked.

"Yep," I said. He turned and went downstairs into his study. I went upstairs to my room. It didn't make sense to say anything else to him. Not then. His eyes had looked too empty, as though he couldn't have found an answer if he'd wanted to. I just had to wait.

On my dresser, there was a picture of the three of us. I stared at it, hearing his voice, then Mom's, then me questioning him again.

Whenever I looked at photographs of the three of us, I was always fascinated by how different our three heads were. Heads, noses, eyes, faces, and hair. It didn't matter where the picture had been taken, whether it was the beach or the living room. It didn't matter if it had been last year or six years ago. It was the three heads, not the bodies or poses—but the heads—that were important. The three heads that were named Ursula, Tim, and Lahni Schuler. Mom's small "peanut head" (as she called it), with her hair like one big, long wave around her small forehead, pointed chin, and brown questioning eyes. Dad's big, wide head covered with thick gray curls, forehead like a TV screen, and gray-blue eyes that made him look like a young kid playing a trick on you that you wouldn't find out about until later.

And there was my head, the smallest, the darkest. Deep brown with other colors too—red and yellow sometimes, depending on the season. Covered by thick, woolly brown hair that also had red in it. My eyes look black to most people, but they're dark brown like the rest of me. My nose has a bump like I've broken it. My mouth is small, and I wish my lips were fuller, rounder. But in every picture since I was ten or so, I'm not smiling and my lips look thin and tight like an old woman's.

The truth is, when I looked at the three heads, I thought how we didn't look like anyone's family. Not really. We didn't look like we belonged together any more than any other three people in the world. I tried to stop myself from thinking it because it seemed so ungrateful to always be considering how we didn't look like a family when my father and mother had tried so hard to make us one. But whenever kids in school talked about separation or divorce, or when Katie was so sure her parents were on the verge, I had started thinking, *We'll be next. I don't know how or why, but I betcha we'll be next. My job is to be ready when it happens.*

Afterward, when I was trying to sleep, the one question I kept hearing my mother ask him was, "Does she know you have a family?" My father hadn't answered. But my mother insisted, "I just want to know if you lie to both of us or only to me. I'm curious, that's all."

Saturday morning my father took his car and left early. I asked my mother if he'd gone back to New York or Germany, but she said, "What he said was that he had business here in town. He said he'd be back." Later she came upstairs and knocked on my door. "If you want to talk to me, you can."

I opened the door and said, "No."

"Well, I'll be here," she said.

She came to my room a couple of hours later. "Honey, are we going to church together tomorrow?"

"Is Dad still going to be here?" *If he is,* I wanted to ask her, *how could you be thinking about that stupid church? Wouldn't you want to be here in the house in case you could make things better? Why would you rather be sitting in church begging for help when you could do something about it yourself by staying home?*

"I don't know if he'll be here or not," she said icily.

"Well, if he's going to be here, *I'm* staying home," I told her.

"Okay," my mother said simply. "If you change your mind . . ."

On Sunday morning I watched Mom drive off by herself, and I waited to hear my father come out of their bedroom. It was almost eleven. When I got down to the kitchen, he was dressed and on the phone, calling a cab.

"Mom said—I thought you were going to be here today."

He came up to me and pulled me to him. I didn't put my arms around him because I didn't want to feel anything. I concentrated on not feeling anything when he hugged me.

"What I told your mom was that I'd stay until this morning. I have to get back to New York, and then I'll fly out tomorrow from there."

"But you can't do any business today. Everything is closed. What are you going to do in New York all day on a Sunday?" I tried to stop myself. Partly because I was afraid of sounding like my mother and partly because I was starting to think like my mother. But I couldn't help it. "Do you have a girlfriend?"

"Lahni, this is not a good idea," my father said sternly. He went to the sink and leaned over it, looking out into the backyard.

"Why can't you just tell me? If it's the truth, why can't you say it?"

He turned back to me, still holding on to the sink. "Because this isn't something you and I should be talking about."

Which meant to me, yes.

He came toward me. I didn't know if he was coming *to* me or trying to get past me, out of the kitchen away from me. I stood still, blocking the doorway. My father stopped in front of me and lifted my face with his hands. "I don't want you to worry, pumpkin. It's going to be okay."

He put his arm around me and walked me into the hallway to where his suitcase was. He opened the door and I followed him out to the end of the driveway. When he reached into his shirt pocket and pulled out a pack of cigarettes, I suddenly felt as if my father had disappeared and been replaced by some other man who looked like him. My father had stopped smoking when I was a baby. He had told me so.

"When did you start smoking again?"

"Oh. I'm sorry, honey. I didn't mean to—I guess I slipped, didn't I?" He put the pack back into his pocket. "Look, we will be okay. We will."

The morning sun was hot, but I knew that wasn't what was making me suddenly drip with sweat. "How could we be okay?" My voice was very loud.

"Lahni, stop!"

"No! *You* should stop. Stop telling me we're going to be okay when you're going to New York to see your girlfriend and coming back on weekends like our house is a hotel!"

I was standing there at the end of our driveway screaming at my father like I'd gone crazy. Other girls screamed at their parents, or so they said. Girls at school bragged about it all the time. But it wasn't what I did, not ever. As much as I honestly meant everything I'd said, I hadn't meant to scream at him. And yet, I couldn't apologize, either. I backed up into the driveway, and as I did, I saw the taxi coming down our street.

Only when I got to the front door did I turn to see my father again. He looked like a kid in his short-sleeved shirt and khaki pants, a very tall boy staring back at me.

I went inside, closed the door, and locked it behind me. I wanted my father to get into the taxi and disappear. *Go wherever you're going,* I thought. *You've probably been wanting to leave for a long time. "We'll be okay." How could you even think to tell me such a big, stupid lie?*

CHAPTER NINE

Gonna get ya high, uh-huh, uh-huh. Gonna make ya holla, uh-huh, uh-huh." Riding my bike from the main building to Sycamore Road, I heard it. I knew immediately who it was because I'd never heard that idiotic song before that first day, and I hadn't heard it since.

I steered my bike as close as I could to the side of the road. I didn't pick up speed and I didn't slow down. I sat and pedaled hard rather than standing up, so my butt wouldn't stick out, swaying back and forth.

"The way you make me feeeall, yeah, got to keep it reaall, yeah." He was so close. He must have been driving very slowly, because I could see Sycamore up ahead, and he still hadn't passed me. I picked up speed. But that's when he picked up speed too. When he drove by me, I saw the back of his head. He had on one of those wool ski hats some of the guys were wearing, even when it was seventy degrees. I didn't see his hair or any of his face, but I knew exactly who it was.

The white Toyota pulled up at the stop sign, but he wasn't signaling left or right. I concentrated on getting to the corner and turning down Sycamore. There's a big sign that says ALL VEHICLES STOP HERE with a picture of a car, a bus, and a bike on it, but I ignored it. I sped right past the Toyota and onto Sycamore Road. The Toyota started down Sycamore behind me. *It's ridiculous to be so bothered by this kid,* I told myself. *You don't even know him. What's the worst he could do? Follow you home and demand you get into his car and make out with him? You're being an imbecile, Lahni. Don't let him scare you.*

I took a shortcut off Sycamore through a field with a bike path. The path led to a dead end, which was our street. I heard Red High-tops, behind me, drive right up to the entrance of the field and stop. I kept going. A few minutes later I heard him back up and screech off down the road.

Red High-tops was gone. The first thing I did was pedal like a maniac right up to my driveway. I looked behind me again before I got off my bike. I ran my bike around the back, leaned it against the house, and didn't even bother to lock it. My hair and forehead were wet with perspiration. Usually I would have started unbuttoning my blouse for air even before I tried the back door to see if it was unlocked. But not this time.

I thought about how no boy had ever asked questions about me or even looked like they might be following me in a car or on foot, not ever. Red High-tops was older than I was; I didn't even know his name, but everything I did know about him made me wish he'd never seen me.

Monday morning I would ask Donna everything she knew about him. Who was he and what did he want? If I had a list of people I had to ask for something, I would have put her name 4,099th on it, but it didn't feel like I had that many choices. So I'd have to go to Donna. She'd be thrilled.

CHAPTER TEN 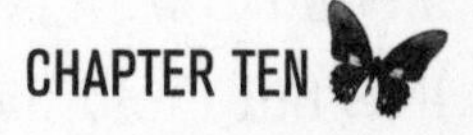

One day Mom wouldn't eat; she'd practically whisper when she said anything at all, and then she'd go to bed at eight. The next day she'd chat nonstop about everything, from the sculpture class she was teaching at the YWCA to how she couldn't wait to do a drastic house-cleaning at the beginning of summer. "Everything from top to bottom gone!" she'd shout, and then repeat it as if it were some kind of magic spell. On those days, I felt sick to my stomach figuring what she was shouting was probably code for my father not living in our house at all by then.

The one thing that seemed pretty consistent was her wanting to go back to Church of the Good Shepherd. Even on the days she was whispering, she'd smile and say, "Lahni, I'm so glad we started going there."

Actually, I was glad too. Not only was I grateful for

something that made her smile, I had also come up with a plan that was centered around Church of the Good Shepherd. So it was good Mom wanted to go back.

When we got to church on Sunday morning, the only thing I could think about was whether Carietta Chisolm would be there. When Marcus Delacroix III started playing the organ and the choir began marching down the aisle, I turned around to see if I could see her. She wasn't in the front of the line, but I told myself not to give up yet because the choir was pretty big. My mom was singing louder and louder with each verse. I thought, *Today's a good day for her. If this is what makes her feel better, then I'm glad I'm here with her.*

All of the women in the choir had passed and now the men were coming. Where was Carietta Chisolm?

They were all marching in time to the music, up to the pulpit where they sat in four rows on either side of Reverend Caffrey. He looked a little less ghostly than he had the last time I was there. I remembered some of the other choir members, especially the two women who'd been sitting on either side of Carietta. Today, though, they were sitting next to each other and she wasn't there.

I suddenly lost interest in being at Church of the Good Shepherd. I was still happy for my mother, but I sulked, staring down at the cover of the program. It had a picture of a dark brown sky with a beam of light shining through it. I took one of the little pencils out of the holder in front of me and started doodling faces over the sky. I knew my mother was probably disappointed that I was scribbling like a preschooler, but it was better than me asking to wait for her in the car.

The minister preached his sermon, the ushers passed the collection plate, and the choir stood to sing their big song for the morning. I stopped doodling to glare at them, still pouting that Carietta wasn't singing with them.

Reverend Caffrey announced, "Here with their own divine message for the morning is our beloved Good Shepherd choir." *Beloved, my foot,* I thought.

Marcus Delacroix's fingers started dancing up and down the keys. And, as if it had been planned exactly this way, a side door up near the pulpit opened, and there was Carietta Chisolm in her navy blue robe with the red satin stole. She hurried over to the choir and slipped into her place.

I glanced at my mother to see if she realized that a miracle had happened. But she was smiling the same smile she'd had since we'd pulled out of our driveway forty-five minutes ago.

Marcus Delacroix began to sing first, in a very high voice about "the rain clouds overhead." I looked at my program again, a little embarrassed that the sky on it was now covered with cartoon figures. The choir started chanting, "Looks like rain, yes, looks like rain." Marcus was standing now over the piano. He sounded like he was crying when he sang, "Can't stand no more rain, what shall I do?" The choir repeated, "Can't stand no more rain, what shall I do?" Then Marcus stopped playing completely. The choir sang "What Shall I Do?" three more times a cappella. Then they stopped too. There was a split second of silence. It was as though the whole church was frozen in sadness, asking the same question.

Suddenly Carietta sang out of the quiet, "Look to that corner of heaven. There's a ray of light shining this way!" I got goose bumps. It was as if she were taking the light she was singing about and guiding it with her voice into the church. My bottom lip started shaking. I folded my hands very tightly in my lap. I was not going to cry.

For the second time, though, Carietta Chisolm had made me stop breathing. I remembered Mr. Faringhelli telling me, "Breathe."

I looked over at my mom. She was prepared this time. She was tearing open a brand-new package of Kleenex. Her nose was red and running.

Not me, I thought. And I wiped my eyes. All right—so they were a little wet. It was for Mom, I told myself. I wanted like anything for a ray of light to shine her way.

Right after the service, I mumbled something to my

mother about finding the ladies' room. She called out after me, "Lahni, I'll come with you," but I was moving too fast.

As soon as I got far enough away from her, I asked a woman if she knew how I could get to where the choir was. She pointed in the direction of the room near the pulpit that Carietta had come out of. The room was locked. I knocked and waited.

Finally an older white woman opened the door.

"I was hoping to see Miss Chisolm," I told her.

"Miss Chisolm?" She looked confused for a moment. "Oh! Carietta! Are you Carietta's little girl?" The woman stood back to get a better look at me. She appeared to be standing in a dark hallway.

"No. I'm not. But I want to speak to her if I could, please."

"Well, she's right back there in the choir room."

I followed her down the hallway. When we got to the end, she opened another door to a room filled with people I recognized from the choir. Across the room, I saw Marcus Delacroix talking with Carietta Chisolm.

"Are you new to the church or are you just visiting?" The woman hadn't stopped smiling except for the one moment she didn't know Carietta Chisolm by her last name.

"Visiting," I said. The woman threw her arm around me suddenly and hugged me so tight, the rooster pin on her dress pinched my forehead.

"Well, welcome, welcome, little visitor. I'm Eileen Miller. Any friend of Carietta's is a friend of mine." She giggled and cooed, "Carietta! Look who I found!"

I was embarrassed when a few people in the room stopped chatting with each other, including Carietta and Marcus Delacroix. Carietta scowled at me, looking puzzled. I looked back at her, not quite believing what I was seeing.

Silver. Silver earrings, silver dress, silver shoes. And a silver rose at the top of her ponytail, which appeared to be even thicker and longer than it was the last time. She looked like the wife of the Tin Man from *The Wizard of Oz*.

Eileen Miller steered me over to her. I tried to smile calmly.

"She was looking for you," Eileen explained, but not enough to erase the scowl from Carietta's face. Eileen patted me on the shoulder and scurried away. I immediately stuck out my hand. "Hi. I'm Lahni Schuler. May I please speak to you when you're not busy, please?" As soon as it came out, I knew I'd said "please" twice. I hadn't meant to sound like I was begging. I was more nervous than I thought.

Carietta studied me for a moment. "You mean right now, today?" She sounded stern, businesslike. Hearing her speak was completely different from hearing her sing. I was so surprised, I wasn't sure how to answer her. Then

I remembered how important my mission was. When else would I have this chance?

"Yes ma'am, today. If it's possible."

Carietta looked at Marcus. "We still goin' out for something to eat?" he asked her. I was sure eating was very important to both of them. I figured Carietta was about to tell me to get lost.

"Oh yes, indeed," she answered him in a husky tone. Turning back to me, she asked, "How long is this gonna take?" She leaned back and stuck her chest out. I kept my eyes on her face—I was sure now that the eyelashes were fake—but I wanted to take a better look at her silver dress. It was cut so low in the front, it made her breasts look like they'd been wrapped in aluminum foil with not enough foil to finish.

"It will only take a second. Really." I felt like I was selling her something, a box of Girl Scout cookies or a raffle ticket.

"Wait for me, you hear?" she commanded Marcus.

Marcus, who was still wearing his choir robe, started to unzip it as he turned to someone else and started another conversation. By now the dark glasses really amused me. Marcus Delacroix III was just cool.

"What can I do for you?" Carietta smoothed the front of her hair back. Her nails were Stoplight Red with perfectly squared tips. Her forehead was high and her hairline so far back that when her hand covered it, she looked like a bald doll with perfect, tan-colored skin and a painted mouth.

"I wanted to ask if you teach voice lessons."

"Voice lessons?" Carietta looked as if I'd asked her something in Russian.

"Yes," I answered. "I thought since you were such a good singer, maybe you gave lessons."

Carietta was still looking at me as if I needed an interpreter. Finally, she said simply, "No. I don't."

I began immediately to back away, feeling silly and embarrassed. "Well, thanks anyway."

Carietta stopped me. "But if you wanna learn how to sing, you should join the choir. Marcus doesn't take on any pupils either far as I know, but he's the best teacher in the city, I guarantee you that."

It had never occurred to me. "Oh—oh," I stammered. "You mean this choir?"

"It's the only choir we have right now. We meet every Thursday night from six to nine. Course I'm sure you've got your homework to do."

I tried to think quickly, but I couldn't. "Well, I do, but I don't think that would be a problem."

"You a good student?" She asked me as though she

were my aunt or some other relative who really cared what the answer was.

"Yes. I am." I answered truthfully and I suppose a little arrogantly. But I'd worked hard to be called a good student. Why should I say anything else?

"That's what I wanted to hear." Carietta lifted her hand royally and caught Marcus's attention a few feet away. "Mar*cus*," she said, putting the emphasis on the last part, which I thought was funny, "would you consider having a new member in the choir? This girl wants to learn how to sing."

Marcus had his choir robe in one hand and the other hand on his hip. He was wearing at least three rings on both hands. He also had on a fluorescent green shirt unbuttoned practically to his navel with a belt to match. Floating on his big chest was a gold chain with an enormous, jeweled cross on it. His pants were solid black. But when I got to his shoes, I had to smile. They matched the shirt and the belt exactly, and they had no backs, but they did have a little heel. Either they were a really large ladies' size, or men wore what my mom called "mules" and I just didn't know it. Between the rings, the shirt, the necklace cross, the satiny green belt, and the mules, I was reasonably sure there was a good chance that Marcus was gay. Now, ask me if I cared. Try *n* for "no." The man was brilliant. All I wanted to do was get into his choir.

"Well," he said, "can she sing already is what I want to know. I don't need anybody else along for the ride."

Why didn't he ask me? I waited to see what Carietta would say.

"Marcus wants to know can you sing already." She patted her hand on her forehead again and then fanned herself, without even looking at me.

I turned and faced Marcus Delacroix III squarely. "Yes, I can sing. I'm in a competition at school, and I want to take lessons to get better. Miss Chisolm suggested I join the choir." I was loud enough that a few people beside Marcus heard me. I realized I might have sounded a little snooty. But I had to show him I could speak for myself, thank you.

Marcus didn't come one step closer. He simply called across to me, "What do you sing?" It was as though I'd entered his kingdom, and I couldn't get closer without a sign or a gesture from him that I was worthy to be there.

But now I was puzzled for a moment. What did I sing? What was he talking about?

"Do you know if you're a soprano or an alto?" Miss Carietta looked at me a little impatiently. I knew she was waiting for this to be over so she could go eat.

"I'm a soprano," I said quietly.

"She's a soprano." Carietta went back to speaking for me as though I'd stepped out of the room.

"We got plenty sopranos. Carietta, for one." I could feel the disappointment down to my toes. Was it too late to say alto or that I'd be happy to sing alto if it meant getting to sing with them? Or tenor? Or bass?

But then Marcus said, "It would be good for you to sit next to Carietta. That'll get you up to speed. Come Thursday night, six o'clock. I don't stand for no lateness, though." He looked hard at Carietta. "That's the only thing I don't think you'll be able to learn from Miss Carietta." Carietta gave him a look like she didn't know what he could be referring to. He snorted, "Huh!"

"Yes, sir," I told him. "I won't be late." Was I nuts? I hadn't even asked my mother if I could join. How humiliating it would be to have to come back to the church and see both of them if my mother said no. Well, she couldn't, that was all. If she was thinking that Good Shepherd was so wonderful, then she'd have to let me join the choir. I probably wouldn't even have to ask my father. I didn't imagine he cared what I did one way or the other these days.

"Thank you," I said to both of them. "Thanks a lot. I'll see you on Thursday." I was in a hurry to get out of there.

It had all happened so fast, and now there was Part Two. Asking Mom.

There weren't that many people left in the church when I came out of the choir room. I went outside and saw my mother up the road standing next to the car. I walked quickly, seeing the worried look on her face.

"Hey," I called.

"What do you mean, 'hey'? I thought you were going to the ladies' room."

"I went to talk to Carietta Chisolm."

My mother's face started to look the same way it had for most of the week, confused and weary. "Who is Carietta Chisolm?"

"She sings in the choir. The one with the ponytail. 'Member today, she came in late and sang the really high part."

"Oh. *Her*! Do you *know* her?" She was obviously very impressed. "What did you want to speak to her about?" Mom still wasn't ready to get in the car. I could tell she wanted an explanation before we left the church.

"I asked her if she taught voice lessons. But she doesn't. She said I should join the choir instead."

"Voice lessons? You never said anything about taking voice lessons. Is that what you want?"

"I did. But now I want to join the choir. Carietta said if

I did, I could learn from Marcus Delacroix. He's the choir director." It sounded, even to me, like an awful lot had happened since I'd left her inside.

"But Lahni, there aren't any other kids in that choir. Are you sure?"

"Yes. I am." It was then that I made the decision not to tell her about the competition until I absolutely had to. If she let me, I'd join the choir and get as good as I could in the next few weeks. It wasn't a lot of time, but combined with Mr. Faringhelli's coaching—for which I'd have to come up with an excuse—just maybe I had a chance at winning.

Mom started to unlock the car door. I knew it was a good sign.

"Lahni, I can't get over this. You never said a word about wanting to study singing before."

"Do you think I have a decent voice?"

"Of course I do. God knows where you get it from. Certainly not from your father or me."

How could she be saying this? It's not as though she knows any more than I do if my real mother or father were good singers. But it was something my mom always did. Speak as though we really were one family, instead of me being part of somebody else's. That's who she was. Somebody who wanted things to be in one piece. She didn't like broken dishes or torn sleeves or books with ripped pages. That's why it was so hard to understand why she'd pick me in the first place. She hated things not to match. Socks, silverware, sheets and pillowcases. If it all didn't fit together perfectly, she didn't want any part of it.

Whenever she talked about the three of us as a family, you could see in her whole body that she truly believed we were. She wouldn't discuss my adoption unless I forced her to. And even then she always looked as if she either wanted to cry or blink her eyes and make me disappear until I'd forgotten there'd ever been an adoption in our family.

"So do you think I could join the choir? It meets on Thursday nights from six to nine. I could definitely make sure my homework was done, so that wouldn't be any big deal."

"That's the only way I'd say yes, Lahni. You're too close to the end of the term to blow it now."

"I won't blow anything, Mom. I promise." I looked over at her. I could see how tired she was, and it made me want to strangle my father. *Why would you marry somebody who wants everything around her to be perfect, if you knew you couldn't live up to it? Sure, maybe nobody could. But knowing you—you probably made her think you could pull it off, you big liar. And now look at her.*

"Honey, you're a good kid and you've worked hard. I want you to do what you think will make you feel good about yourself."

Yeah, I wanted to say to her. *That's exactly what I was thinking about you.*

CHAPTER ELEVEN

"You tell her! You come here and tell her yourself. If you think I'm going to do your dirty work for you, you're crazy!"

Of course, I knew who my mother was shouting at on the phone at one o'clock in the morning.

"No! You do what is right, Tim. You come here and you tell her yourself."

I ran out into the hall, half-knowing what she was saying. She was demanding that my father come home and tell me himself that he was divorcing her, instead of leaving it to her to tell me. I'd been waiting for this for weeks. Now that it was here, I didn't need him to come home and tell me anything. My mother's voice had already told me what I needed to know.

I waited outside their bedroom until she hung up.

"Mom?"

"I'm sorry I woke you up, Lahni. Do you want to come in?"

She was sitting on the side of the bed, looking at me calmly. I stepped inside the room but no farther.

"What are you two going to do?"

"Your father is going to come home and talk to you."

"Can't you tell me now? Are you getting a divorce?"

She continued to look at me, and slowly her lips turned up into a sad smile.

"Looks like it, Lahni. I'm sorry. I really am."

"I know," I told her. I went to her and put my arms around her. She didn't move.

After a moment, I put my hand on the top of her head and felt the hardness of her skull under her hair.

"You'll be okay, Mom," I told her. "You'll be fine."

I went to school determined not to think about my parents' divorce. Instead, I immediately got into a conversation with Donna Thoren about Red High-tops. Katie and I went to her locker and waited until she got there. We didn't think there was much chance she'd be alone, but, luckily for us, not even one member of The Pack was with her when she came down the hall.

It turned out, though, she didn't know anything about

Red High-tops except she thought he was in tenth grade. "I'm always around the Kent guys," she bragged, "and if I don't know who he is, he's probably some loser who doesn't have any friends."

"Well, who was he with when he asked you about me?"

"That's what was so weird about it," she said. "I didn't even see him at first. He must have been watching me talk to these other guys who are always trying to get me to drive around with them. He just came over and said, 'What's the black girl's name in your class?' I told him. And he kind of laughed. He said, 'I wonder what she looks like without any clothes on.'"

I didn't need to hear her repeat *that* again. "Can you please find out what his name is?"

Donna laughed. "So you *do* think he's cute!"

"No. That's not it at all. I want to know because I think he's after me, and I at least want to know what his name is."

"What do you mean, 'after you'?"

I knew I'd said too much already. Donna Thoren had a very big mouth, and if she started spreading what I'd said around, she could make things a lot worse.

"All I meant was, I'm not sure why he would want to know anything about me. I'd never even seen him before the day you pointed him out. But I'm sure it's no big deal."

But it was Katie who blurted out, "Of course, it's a big deal! He's *stalking* you, like a maniac!"

That's all Donna needed to hear. "Really?" She stared at me, wild-eyed. "*Stalking* you? I'm sure I can find out who he is, Lahni. I can't believe he's stalking you! Whoaaa!"

I couldn't have been sorrier that Katie and I had waited for her that morning. I'd spent a couple of years making sure Donna and The Pack knew as little as possible about me. Now that she finally had something on me, I was sure everyone at Darby would find out as soon as she could get it around.

That afternoon when I got home from school my mother announced, "Your father's calling you tonight. He said to make sure you were here between six and seven."

By seven forty-five, I was past nervous. I was furious. What the heck did he think he was doing? I decided the next time I saw him, I wouldn't listen to anything he wanted to say. I'd tell him how badly I thought he'd treated Mom. I'd say I was happy they were getting a divorce because now maybe she'd have a chance to find someone who deserved her. I'd tell him I didn't want to see him afterward, so he shouldn't even try to persuade me.

The phone rang. I waited to see if my mother would

pick it up downstairs in the kitchen. I certainly wasn't going to jump to answer it after waiting an hour for his call.

The phone rang again. I went and opened the door of my room to listen.

"Lahni," my mother called from the foot of the stairs. "It's your father, honey."

I walked as slowly as I could into her room and picked up the phone. "Yes?"

"Lahni?" *Lame,* I thought. *The first word ought to be "sorry."*

"I know I'm calling a little later than I said. I was in a meeting that lasted longer than I guessed it would."

I didn't answer.

"Lahni?"

"What did you want to speak to me about?"

"I want to come home this weekend to see you. I want us to talk."

"If you're going to tell me you're getting a divorce, you don't have to come home to do it. I already know."

"Lahni, would you give me a break here? I want us to sit down and talk. You and me. Can we do that, please?" I realized how odd it was to hear him use the word "please." My father didn't usually ask for things. He told you what he wanted done.

"Are you coming for the whole weekend?"

"No. I'm coming on Saturday. In the afternoon. I thought we could talk then."

"So you're only coming to speak to me and then you're leaving?"

"Yes."

I understood then that he might never spend another night in our house. He was disappearing. The talk this weekend was one more step toward him erasing himself from us.

"So I guess I'll see you then."

"Saturday, Lahni. At about one o'clock. I'll pick you up."

I knew then that he probably wasn't even coming inside. It was an appointment he'd made with his daughter to say what? That he was sorry and hoped we would still be close? And then he'd be gone again. So, fine.

"Bye, Dad." I tried to sound as casual as possible. I wanted to get used to sounding casual. Like I didn't know when I'd see him again and that was all right with me.

He said, "I'll see you Saturday, Lahni." And he was gone.

CHAPTER TWELVE

Onyx 1. That's what he tells people to call him. But his name is Harry Tiboldt. Isn't that awful? Wouldn't you come up with something else if your name was Harry Tiboldt? I know I would. Anyway, he's a junior. Pretty quiet, but smart. And waaaay into hip-hop. Brad says he positively thinks he's a black guy." Donna was practically breathless spouting the information. As usual, she was doing it so that any girl in the hall within twenty feet of us could hear it too. "Doesn't it make sense now why he's checkin' you out? I mean, since he thinks he's black?"

Katie made this vomiting sound she always does if someone says something particularly stupid or offensive. Donna gave her a look of total dismissal.

I smiled and said, "Thanks a lot for telling me, Donna," and started to move on.

"Should I tell Brad to tell him you think he's cute?"

"No, please," I told her. "I just wanted to know what his name is, that's all."

"At least, now you'll prob'ly have a date for the mixer, if nobody else asks you." Donna waited a second for my reaction, then moved along down the hall.

"I can't believe what an imbecile she is," Katie said, not caring how loud she was.

I immediately turned and started the other way, even though we all should have been going in the same direction. Katie came with me.

"Are you worried because of that day he was driving so weird next to us while we were riding our bikes?" she asked.

"He did it twice. And believe me, the second time was a lot weirder than the first."

"Really?" Katie sounded concerned, but I knew she was also probably happy I was confiding in her.

"I thought I should at least find out what his name is."

"Do you think?—"

"I don't want to talk about it anymore, Katie." She kept walking next to me, but I knew her feelings were hurt now. Even so, it was all I was going to tell her.

A few minutes later she asked, "Did you decide if you're going to sing in the talent competition?"

"Yep. I am."

Katie smiled so big I knew I was forgiven for not wanting to talk about Onyx 1 or Harry Tiboldt or whatever the jerk's name was. "You'll probably win."

I knew she really hoped that was true. I thought, *It's so interesting to know someone who believes in other people like she does. Wait,* I almost wanted to tell her, *till you find out how the closest people to you can be the biggest letdowns of all."*

The next time I saw Onyx 1 was Thursday, the first night of my choir practice at Good Shepherd. Katie and I were at the bike rack, ready to head home. I was nervous, wondering if I'd really be good enough to sing in the choir. The idea of sitting next to Carietta Chisolm and letting her hear me was so terrifying I had to laugh. Katie took the grin on my face to mean I was in a particularly good mood. "You must be thinking about the competition, huh, Lahni?" she teased.

"Kind of," I answered. "In a way."

We got on our bikes and headed down the Darby entrance road. When we got to the end, we stopped before turning onto Sycamore. Just as we were about to pull off, a noisy red jeep came down from Kent and pulled up next to us.

"Hey y'all!" a voice yelled over the music. I turned and

saw all of them at the same time. Donna was in the back of Brad Tarleton's jeep. Brad was driving. Next to him, under a red and black striped ski hat with a toothpick hanging out of his mouth, was Onyx 1. He stared at me without any particular expression that I could tell, and I stared back.

His face was thin, pale, and doughy. But his lips were big and red looking, as though he'd just bitten them. There was a purplish scar just below his mouth, like someone had accidentally drawn a line across his chin with a crayon or marker. Most of his hair was up under the ski cap, but what was showing was thick and brown, bushy like a curly broom.

He didn't stop looking at me and I didn't stop looking at him.

Finally, I made myself say hi to Donna.

"This is Brad and this is Onyx 1!" Donna called to us gaily. I could tell she was watching me for a reaction. I was trying to look tough, like he shouldn't even think about trying to harass me.

Brad was silent, but Onyx 1 smiled, pulled the toothpick out of his mouth, pursed his lips, and made the same clicking sound he'd made before at me. I squinted but tried to keep focused on him, trying to tell him he didn't scare me and the last thing I thought was that he was cute.

I tried to look like I thought he was repulsive. Then Brad drove off onto Sycamore Road.

Katie watched them all disappear before she asked me, "What do you think Donna told him?"

"I don't know." I started pedaling down Sycamore. "But what could I do about it even if I knew?"

"What was that thing he was doing, that weird sound?"

"Katie, I don't know!!" Why didn't she get it? How could I explain what this kid was doing? It didn't make any more sense to me than it did to her. He was nuts, crazy, trouble. The last thing I needed was a white boy who called himself Onyx 1 following me in his car and making noises at me when he saw me. I didn't know what to do about it or who to tell. The only thing I knew was that I wanted it to stop.

CHAPTER THIRTEEN

"Y'all better start singin' like you got something to sing about! We can't inspire anybody else to lift up their hearts, if we're singin' like our own are stuck to the soles of our shoes." We were learning the music for a song we were supposed to perform on Sunday. Even though I was concentrating on remembering the soprano part as I was singing it, I thought the choir sounded great around me. Obviously, Marcus didn't think so. He walked around each section and listened to it. He sang each part with them as he did, going from soprano to bass in an instant. "That's not it," he'd snap. Then he'd sing the part. "That's what you should be singing!"

When he stopped in front of me, I sang louder, still trying to blend with the rest of the sopranos but also wanting Marcus to know that I wasn't afraid of him hearing me. If I was going to use my singing in the choir to get better for the competition, now was no time to be timid. Marcus stood for a long time in front of me, listening. I couldn't tell what he thought, because he didn't say anything, didn't change his expression at all. He seemed to have two of them—stone-faced and frowning, except when he talked to Carietta about food or when he was playing the piano or organ. When he was playing, he looked as if he were someplace in his mind where he could hear our voices, but there was no other human being there but him. And when he talked about food, he looked like he was almost in the same place as when he played music.

"I don't know, y'all," he grumbled. "You shouldn't really be singin' this kind of music if it don't touch you someplace personal. Then you s'posed to share it. But you can't share what you don't have, can you?" He shook his head sorrowfully. "Now, the choir will be singing the chorus, and I want three voices on the verse in harmony. That'll be Carietta on the high part, Lizzie—you sing the second soprano part, and I'll do the tenor."

Marcus sat down at the piano and played an

introduction. Then he nodded, and he and Carietta began to sing.

"There's no way for me to move a mountain
No way that I can see.
I can't change the world's cold heart
Hard as I try
So I figure
I'll just let it be."

Marcus stopped playing. He stood up, slid his dark glasses down so I could see his eyes, and glared at me in the front row of the soprano section. "What happened to you, Miss Lizzie?"

As usual when I was nervous, I stopped breathing for a second, then I answered as steadily as I could. "I'm sorry, Marcus. I didn't know you meant me. My name's Lahni. You said 'Lizzie'."

Marcus continued to glare at me for a minute before his face changed slowly and he began to laugh huskily. "So I did. Well, c'mon, Miss Lahni. We need your voice in here, little sister."

He was already playing the intro again. When he was almost finished, he looked up from the keyboard and winked at me. I began to sing with the two of them. I wasn't even sure what the second soprano part was, but I heard what Marcus and Carietta were singing and tried to harmonize with them. I was lower than Carietta but higher than Marcus. When we finished the verse, the choir started.

"Somehow the clouds unfold
And I hear a trumpet roll
And I know that somebody else is in charge!"

We did the whole song and we all finished together; Marcus continued for a few measures before he played like he was trying to bust the keys loose from the rest of the piano. When he stopped, people in the choir shouted, "Amen!" Carietta leaned over to me and said, "All right, all right now girl!"

Marcus got up slowly from the piano, back to his stone face. "Thank you, choir. Now I can hear why somebody bothered to write this song." He looked at me and Carietta. "Ladies, that was very nice." He smiled. "I'm glad we got little sister's name right, so we could have the pleasure of that very righteous second soprano." I thought my lips would stretch out, I was grinning so wide. *So, I'm okay,* I thought. *Whoooeee! Hallelujah! Marcus Delacroix thinks I'm okay!*

CHAPTER FOURTEEN

I'd never seen my father nervous before. About anything. His voice was trembly. His breath smelled of cigarettes and Listerine strips. When he said my name, it was in a whisper. But he was bluffing, trying to act as if he wasn't nervous at all. He was trying to talk to me like I was one of his computer designers. He was an executive; I was an employee.

"I'm glad we could meet, just the two of us. It's better if you and I discuss this alone. I think we've always had good communication between the two of us, don't you?"

I bit the inside of my lip. He looked very handsome in his salmon-colored knit sports shirt and his khakis. I'd never seen the shirt before; I'd never seen him wear a color like salmon. He wore white and pale blue and sometimes navy blue, but that was it. What was more surprising, shocking really, were the sandals. It was May, all right, and at school we'd already been reminded we couldn't wear flip-flops to class. But I'd never seen my father wear anything in the spring and summer but sneakers. Even when we went to the beach, he'd wear his old, ripped up sneakers without laces. But he hadn't owned any sandals that I knew of. The ones he had on today were just like flip-flops, except in leather, so his hairy feet were out where everyone could see them. What had happened to him—so quickly?

"You look so different."

"Naw. I do? How so, honey?"

"I've never seen you wear a color like that." I nodded my head toward his shirt. "And you have on sandals."

"Don't you like them?"

"I just think it's weird that you're changing everything. So fast."

"Lahni, you're being silly. I have on a new shirt and sandals. Those aren't what I'd call significant changes."

"Considering you bought them after you moved out, and I've never seen you dress this way before, I'd say they are pretty significant."

"Excuse me," my father said sternly. He put up two fingers in the air to get the waitress's attention. He'd picked me up at home without coming inside and driven us downtown to a fancy restaurant called Strawberry Fields. I was the youngest person in the room and the only black one. My father was the only man. It was filled with women my mother's age and older. They hadn't stopped staring at my father and me since we'd come in. It was as though we had invaded a luncheon for white women only and nobody had the courage to tell us.

"You say I moved out and I guess I have. Your mother and I agreed it would be the best thing for everyone if I stayed in New York. So I got a place. It's actually in a hotel, because I'm in and out of the country so much. But the important thing is, it has a room for you, hon, because I want you to be able to come and visit when you want to."

When I'd want to? At that moment, I couldn't imagine when that would be.

"Because it's a hotel, you won't be able to decorate exactly, but we can definitely buy some things so that you feel like it's yours."

"Does your girlfriend live there?" I couldn't help it. Knowing about her was the only other important thing to me, other than him leaving my mother. I wanted to know who he thought was better than she was for him. Who did he think was more attractive, who did he want to sleep with more than my mom?

"Lahni"—now he was unable to hide the quivering

in his voice at all—"I'm not going to lie to you. I do have a . . . friend. She's a really good friend, but we don't have any plans for anything more than that."

Now that he'd finally said it, I wished I owned a cell phone like everyone else so I could call my mother and say, *I don't know if he had the guts to admit it to you yet, but he just told me. There is somebody. They're not getting married according to him—he calls her a "really good friend"—but there definitely is somebody.*

"Lahni, I know you're probably really angry with me—"

"I'm just glad that you're finally admitting it to me."

"But honey, that's not why your mother and I are separating."

"You mean you having a girlfriend?"

"Yes, Lahni." I could tell he was struggling to have this conversation. He didn't like explaining himself. He had always said, "I don't have to explain myself to you, Lahni." I knew how much he must hate this moment. "Me having a friend is not the reason your mother and I are getting a divorce."

Why was he such a liar? Didn't he think I'd heard him go from saying "separating" to "divorce" in less than a minute?

"You didn't answer me, Dad. Does your girlfriend live with you?" I wasn't sure that I hated him, but I felt pretty close.

"No. Of course not. I wouldn't be telling you there was a room for you to stay in if that were the case. You may think I'm a monster, Lahni, but I'm not."

He was wrong. I didn't have a name for him and I wasn't sure I hated him. But he definitely *felt* like an enemy. He'd already proved he was a liar. And he had a girlfriend even though he wasn't divorced. No, not a monster. But definitely an enemy of my mother's and mine.

"I was hoping you'd come next weekend. For the afternoon. Sunday afternoon. I'd pick you up and bring you back. I already asked your mom. She said if it was all right with you, it was fine with her."

What else do you think she'd say, butthead? She probably can't stand looking you in the face anymore. Why are you asking her anything?

"I have to think about it." The waitress had finally come to take our order, and I was so nauseous, all I wanted to do was get home fast so I could throw up.

"What do you want to eat, Lahni?"

"I don't have any appetite, Dad. I want to go home, please." I didn't have any problem looking at him. I wanted him to see how much I didn't want to be there with him.

He paused for a minute, staring at me. The waitress

stood at his side, looking down at us. Finally my father said, "Well, that's it then." He looked up at the waitress. "I guess we won't be staying."

When she'd gone, he said, "Lahni, this whole thing won't be easy for any of us. I haven't been able to eat for a few nights myself."

I stood up, ready to leave. Slowly he got up also. When I turned around, I could see women from tables all over the room watching us. What's that young black girl doing with that white man? Sure, it had happened before, but I never felt it do so many different things to my body at the same time as it did when I was walking out of Strawberry Fields. I wanted to stop in the middle of the restaurant, pick up a microphone, and tell all of them very calmly, "You wanna know what the story is? He used to be my father. We came here to this lovely restaurant so he could let me know he's giving up the job."

If I'd felt he was still my dad, I would have wanted to surprise him, like I was surprising Mom, with my singing at Church of the Good Shepherd the next day. No matter what he felt about church, if he was still my dad, I know he would have wanted to come.

But as we walked past their tables, my father felt to me exactly like what the women in Strawberry Fields were seeing. A curly haired white man in a salmon-colored shirt, khakis, and sandals leaving an expensive restaurant with a fourteen-year-old black girl.

When we got to the middle of the floor, I felt my father reach for me. I looked down to see that he was holding out his hand to me. I looked up at him and put both my hands in my pockets. I saw how it hurt him, but it hurt me, too. I walked out ahead of him, by myself.

CHAPTER FIFTEEN

Just before we sang, Carietta lifted the cross on the chain around her neck and kissed it. "C'mon little sister, let's tear it up," she whispered to me. We stood with the rest of the choir and began to step-touch to Marcus's playing. I wasn't much of a dancer, but I definitely liked this step-touch move. Eventually I added a little sway and bob with my head.

When it was time for Marcus, Carietta, and me to sing our special part, I purposely didn't look in my mother's direction. I wanted to see the expression on her face when she heard me, but I knew it would come as more of a shock if I wasn't even looking at her when we started. I wanted my singing to look like it was nothing so unusual. It was such a casual thing that I'd forgotten to mention it.

I sang louder than I'd ever sung before in my life. I wanted to prove to Marcus that he hadn't made a mistake by picking me. I looked at Carietta as if to say, *Aren't I singing this better than you expected?* and the look she gave me back made me know everything was definitely not all right. I knew I was singing the right notes and I'd come in with the two of them at the right time. What could possibly be the matter? I looked at Marcus and I couldn't see his eyes, but I didn't have to. He looked like he'd just bitten into a bug sandwich, but I still didn't know why. When the three of us had done our part, the choir continued and we all finished together.

Finally I looked out at my mom, and she was looking at me too like I'd suddenly grown another nose. What was it? What had I done wrong?

Carietta didn't say anything to me all through the service. Marcus wouldn't have been able to if he wanted to, because he was so far away from the choir. But when we went back to what the choir called the robe room—the room where I had first met the two of them—I waited to hear why they seemed so upset.

When both of them were back there and neither one had said anything to me, I decided I'd ask. How could I learn how to do better if they didn't tell me what I'd done wrong? I looked across the room. They were standing together laughing, bend-over-and-slap-your-thigh laughing. Now I was disgusted. I couldn't believe it. I was the kid; they were the so-called adults. How could they be laughing at me for making a mistake my first time singing with them? If it was anybody's fault, it was Marcus's. He was the one who'd told me to sing the stupid part in the first place.

Swallowing hard, with my throat dry and aching, I turned to leave. I just wanted to get out of their dumb church as fast as possible. When I got to the door, Marcus called out, "Where you going, little sister?"

I turned back, sullenly. I could feel the other choir members watching. What was he going to do now—try to embarrass me even more in front of them?

"Come here, girl." Carietta stood next to him, still smiling.

I decided whatever he had to say, I would listen and then leave. No matter who laughed, I'd be fine. It was the two of them who were rude and mean, not me.

"Yes?" I clenched my jaw.

"Little sister, you sang today like you were on fire, girl! I was so stupefied from the sound comin' outta your little frame, I had to look twice to see if it was really you."

It was *me* who was stupefied—was he serious or was he mocking me?

Carietta said, "I was standing right next to you. Shoot, I had to grip my heels so I wouldn't fly out my shoes!" The whole room laughed. But when they did, I knew it was a good laugh, not one that meant I was the joke. I was able to laugh with them, and their faces told me they admired what I'd done. I stood there feeling hot throughout my whole body.

Marcus bent down and his smile disappeared. Instead there was the familiar stone face. "But I want you to remember something." His voice was so soft, he was almost whispering, and he was so close I could smell a mix of cologne and hair oil. Behind his glasses, his eyes focused on mine. "What you did today was good. *Real* good. There's no doubt about it. And I mean to give you a chance to show folks you can sing solo." He drew back a few inches and studied my face. I'd heard what he said about singing solo, but I knew from his tone that whatever was coming next was the most important part. "But you got to learn how to sing in a group, though. How to share the sound and don't make it all about your own voice. You understand what I'm sayin'?" And I did. I hadn't *meant* to sing louder than both of them; I hadn't really thought it was possible. I just wanted to make sure he could *hear* me, that *everybody* could hear me. But I understood what he was saying to me, and I'd prove it to him.

"Yes sir, I understand."

He stood up straight again. "And don't be callin' me no 'sir.' I may look like somebody's ol' grandpapa, but I ain't." He leaned back and hooted. So did Carietta and the rest of the choir.

When I got outside, my mother was waiting for me. I could tell by the raccoon circles of mascara that she'd been crying. But everything else in her face told me how proud she was.

"Well, there should be no doubt in anybody's mind what a fine singer my daughter is," she said as we walked to the car. "Do you know what you did to me in there? I was a mess, a complete mess."

"Yeah." I smiled. "I can see it. Especially around the eyes."

When we got into the car, just before she drove out of the parking lot, she asked without looking at me, "Did you tell your father you were going to sing today?"

"No," I said quietly, not looking at her either.

"Wouldn't you have wanted him to be here?" Now I felt her staring, watching my face for the answer.

"No," I said. I was pretty sure I wasn't lying. "Not really." And I tried not to think of what he would have looked like sitting there beside her or if he would have liked what I'd done. Or if it might have made him think twice about giving us up.

CHAPTER SIXTEEN

I don't know what you're doing, but whatever it is, keep it up!" Mr. Faringhelli liked what he heard when I went for my coaching. I told him, though, that I wasn't sure I still wanted to sing "When Will I Know That I'm Home?" for the competition. After what had happened to me on Sunday morning, I wasn't in the mood to sing anything that made me seem sad and pitiful.

"You can sing anything you choose, Lahni. But you don't have a lot of time to fool around making a decision. We only have a couple of weeks till the competition. It's a little late to be picking a new song."

"I'll have one next coaching," I told him. I knew what I was going to do. My plan was to ask Marcus to choose something for me on Thursday at choir practice. He knew my voice as well as Mr. Faringhelli did. Maybe, after Sunday, he knew it better. I was sure he could come up with something that would make me feel like I had a chance, at least, of winning.

When I left the classroom, Donna and Amber were waiting in the hall right outside. Amber whined, "You sounded soooo good. I don't even know why I'm staying in the competition, you sounded so good." I couldn't believe they'd been eavesdropping on my coaching.

"I've got something for you," Donna told me. "And I promised I wouldn't leave the building until I put it in your hands." When she held the folded piece of paper out toward me, my good mood disappeared instantly. They both stood there waiting for me to open it. If I could have thought of some way to get out of it, I would have, but I couldn't. So I opened it in front of them, holding the paper so that neither one of them could read whatever it said.

Onyx 1 + U. U=MINE

In red pen. That was it. I tried not to have any expression on my face as I calmly folded the paper back up. "Thanks, Donna," I said.

"Well? What did he say?" she wanted to know.

"Didn't you read it?" It occurred to me both she and Amber probably had since it wasn't in a sealed envelope.

"No, of course I didn't," Donna said, bugging her eyes

out, trying to look as though she wasn't capable of such a thing.

"Neither did I," whined Amber. Her acting was worse than Donna's.

I shrugged and faked a smile. "It's so dumb. Not even worth repeating." Then I walked slowly down the hall away from them, hoping they wouldn't follow me.

As soon as I got through the hallway doors, I realized my hand was so sweaty around the note, it felt like a piece of chewed gum. But I waited until I got all the way outside the building before I opened it again.

Onyx 1 + U. U=MINE

He was an idiot, a wacko. Who else but a wacko would send a person a note like this and yet not even speak to them when they saw them in person? No, he was crazy and I wanted him to go away. I kept thinking about the "naked" crack. What kind of a guy says that about a girl to another girl? Was it just because I didn't have any experience that I thought it was nuts? Or was I right to be afraid of him?

I looked at the note one last time. I told myself, if it freaks you out that much, don't look at it. But I didn't throw it away. I put it in the front pocket of my backpack, and even though it was a tiny piece of paper, I felt like it had suddenly made my backpack about a hundred pounds heavier.

CHAPTER SEVENTEEN

On the way to the city, there was mostly silence. It was as though my father and I were sitting in the front of the car and the ghosts of us as a family were in back. I would have been fine with letting them stay there, but my father was determined to pretend our family wasn't dead exactly, just not quite alive.

"What's going on with you . . . I mean, in school?" he asked.

"Nothing . . . special," I told him.

He frowned. "Aren't you getting ready for middle school graduation? Is that what they call it? Graduation?"

"Mostly the school calls it that. The kids just talk about getting out of middle school."

"But there's a ceremony, right? When is it? In June?"

"Yeah. June tenth."

"Is it a formal thing?"

"What do you mean by 'formal'?"

He said, "What I *mean* is, if you and your mother need to go shopping for a dress or anything . . ."

I just waited. When he didn't finish, I said, "What, Dad? If we have to go shopping, what?"

"Lahni, give me a break here, would you? Your mother and I haven't had a chance to talk about it, so I'm trying to let you know I'll do whatever you want me to—"

"I don't want you to do anything, Dad. We're supposed to wear white for graduation, so no, I don't have a white dress. And yes, I'm gonna have to get one. But I talked it over with Mom and it's all taken care of." That was a lie. My mother and I hadn't talked about graduation at all. I just wanted to make him feel bad, like he'd already been left out of something because he wasn't around.

I never mentioned the stuff that was important to me. Not singing in church, not the middle school competition, and definitely not Onyx 1. If things had been good between my father and me, he certainly would have heard about Onyx 1 by now. If my father had known about any of it—the note, the times Onyx 1 followed me in his car, and him saying he wondered what I looked like naked—he would have gone crazy. By the time my father would have finished with Onyx 1, if he was even still at

Kent, Onyx 1 would definitely be turning in the opposite direction if he happened to see me.

"Dad, there really isn't any big deal about graduation. I am just getting out of middle school. But I really don't know if I'll be able to come see you in New York again until the school year is over. I'm trying to keep my grades up, and I'm trying to look out for Mom too."

"What do you mean 'look out' for her? What exactly is going on?"

"Dad, are you serious? Do you think she's just going along with the flow, like everything in our house hasn't completely changed? My getting out of middle school is the least of it. You don't know that?" I was trying to keep my voice as calm sounding as possible.

"Lahni, your mother and I are adults. We can take care of ourselves. You shouldn't have to be some kind of nurse for her because things aren't going so well between us."

"I'm not being a nurse for her. I'm trying to be her friend." I didn't care at that point what he thought of my tone. How could he tell me about Mom being able to take care of herself? At least she hadn't run out and got herself a boyfriend. Was the woman he was calling his "really good friend" his idea of taking care of himself?

When we got to the city, Dad stopped talking to me and started cursing under his breath at the other drivers.

When we got to Sixty-fourth Street, though, he said, "Well, whadda ya know!" and grinned. "See Lahni"—he reached over and pinched my nose—"you're my good luck!" It was something he'd told me since I was a little girl, but he hadn't said it in months. I saw the parking space he was so happy to get, but I didn't see any building near it that looked like a hotel. There was no awning that announced it, no bellboys running in and out with suitcases.

We got out and went down Sixty-fourth Street to the middle of the block. When we got to the entrance of the Mayfair Hotel, I thought it looked like a huge apartment house. It did have bellboys and its name was printed on the floor of the lobby, but it was in very small letters. Anyone could have easily missed it. I'd heard my mother accusing my father of preferring to live in an expensive hotel rather than at home, but I couldn't have told her if she was right about the expensive part, because I hadn't been in very many hotels.

Central Park was across the street. I imagined my father picked his hotel because it was near the park. He always talked about jogging in our neighborhood and playing tennis like he used to, but he was barely home long enough to change his shoes. Did he jog now, with his girlfriend? Did they play tennis together? Did he find time now that he lived in New York across the street from Central Park?

It seemed that since my father had announced to me he was leaving, I'd become more sensitive to people staring at us as though we looked peculiar together. From the time we got out of the car, I felt like we were freaks—everyone looked as though they wanted to know the story of who we were and why we were together. In the Mayfair lobby, my father walked past the desk, waving to the man behind it. Then suddenly he stopped, turned back, and guided me to it. "Robert, this is my daughter, Lahni. You remember I said I was bringing her into the city for the afternoon. Lahni, this is Robert."

"Hello, miss," the man behind the desk said.

"Hello," I answered. I could feel my father's hand grip my shoulder. He turned me around and we walked to the elevator together. *I guess you don't bother to tell the man at the front desk in a hotel that your daughter's adopted. You just let him wonder.*

My father lived on the sixteenth floor of the Mayfair. His apartment, as he insisted on calling it, was number 1601. It was decorated in the exact opposite style of our house in New Clarion. There was a little hallway with a huge, gold-framed mirror, and then a living room, I guess you'd say, with red and gold wallpaper. Immediately I thought of how much my mother would hate it.

Our house was all shades of blue, a color Mom called

"seafoam," and her favorite, pearl gray. She was always telling my father that if she changed anything in the house and he wasn't comfortable with it, it was important that he tell her. Eventually what he told her was that he was tired of hearing her say that, and if he had a problem, he definitely would let her know. After we knew he was leaving, I asked her if she was sorry she'd tried so hard to please him. She laughed and said it was the same as asking if she was sorry she'd tried to please me. I didn't think it was the same at all. I still don't. But I didn't argue it with her. Actually, she asked me not to, because she could tell from my face how much I disagreed.

My father went right to the doorway of a room off a tiny kitchen. "This is the room I told you about," he said. "This is yours." It was at that exact moment that I think we both heard the water running from what must have been the bathroom. It stopped, someone coughed or cleared her voice, and a door opened down the hall. We both looked in that direction.

When I saw the woman's face, I knew immediately who she was. At the same time, I couldn't believe it was actually happening.

"Hello!" she said brightly, although there was shock all over her face. "I'm Pat." She came right toward me with her hand out. She was wearing a long white bathrobe that was so thick it could have been a parka. She had very black hair, dyed, I was pretty sure. It was wet and shiny like a seal's back. Girls in school dyed their jet hair black to look goth. I didn't know what her excuse could be.

"I'm Lahni," I said, but I didn't stick out my hand.

"I didn't think you'd be back so early, Tim," she said to my father nervously. "I didn't think I'd still be here when you got back."

"I didn't think so either," he said sourly.

She looked as though he'd slapped her.

"I'm going downstairs," I said.

"Lahni!" my father barked. But I kept walking. He was right behind me when I got out to the hallway. "What are you doing?"

I stopped. "I'm going home," I told him, without looking at him.

"Don't be ridiculous," he said. "Pat wasn't supposed to be here, and now she's leaving."

I faced my father. "But she doesn't have to, Dad. *I* am."

"I know that you're upset, but it was a mistake. *Her* mistake. I did want you to meet her, eventually, but not today. Today it was supposed to be just us."

"Dad, I really want to go home. I can take the train. It's easy."

"I don't want you to go." It sounded like an order with a whine mixed in.

I stood there trying to decide if I had the courage to turn away from him and keep walking to the elevator. I wasn't used to disobeying my father. I was used to doing whatever he said, and most of the time, without giving him any of what he called "lip." But I knew I wasn't going back into the room with that woman, either. I took a deep breath and sort of propelled myself toward the elevator. I pushed the button to take me to the lobby.

"Lahni, you're not taking any train!"

"Then I'll call Mom. She'll come get me."

"This is not right. In a few minutes Pat will be gone and we can—" The elevator door opened. There were three other people in it. I stepped in and so did my father. Again I could feel people looking at us. At first neither of us said anything. Then my father very quietly said, "Why don't we go get a soda or something and talk about this?"

I looked up at him but I didn't answer. When the doors opened to the hotel lobby, I stepped out and started looking around for a pay phone.

"Lahni, what about my suggestion?"

"I'm going to call Mom," I repeated.

"And we can't even talk about it?" I just kept looking around the lobby. My father sighed loudly. "Well, if you're so determined to go right back, *I'll* drive you."

I knew that wasn't going to happen if I could help it.

Being in that hotel and seeing that woman in the bathrobe made me realize what I guess my mother knew. My father was already part of a totally different world. A world I didn't want any part of. I wanted to either take the train or have my mother come get me. I wanted to get away from my father as soon as I could, not ride in a car with him for an hour.

"I'm sorry," he said. "I really am."

I looked up at him and back down again. I thought about stupid Pat with her wet black hair, looking like she'd been caught robbing my father's apartment. I wished that's exactly what had happened. That we'd caught her stealing and now he knew what an idiot he'd been. He'd have to beg my mother's forgiveness and mine, too, for being so dumb.

"I have to find a phone," I told him.

He pointed to the other side of the lobby, looking like it was the last thing he wanted to do. "I wish you wouldn't do this. Asking your mother to drive here and back."

"She won't mind," I answered. For the first time I tried to figure out what I really *would* say. That we'd gone to my father's hotel and his girlfriend was there, and I didn't want to stay, even if she left? That was the truth, but how could I tell my mother that?

My father gave me his credit card for the phone call.

He sat in the lobby staring at me. I turned around after I dialed so I could have some privacy.

While the phone was ringing, I kept trying to decide whether to tell the truth. By the time I heard my mother's voice, I'd made up my mind.

"Mom?"

"Honey, are you all right? Where are you?"

"I'm in the lobby of Dad's hotel."

"Where's your father, Lahni?" I could tell she was already upset and I hadn't even begun.

"He's here, Mom. I mean, not right here. He's sitting . . . across the room."

"Lahni, what's the matter? You sound strange."

I could feel my throat closing up. I'd be mad at myself if I started to cry. "Mom, I know it's a lot to ask, but do you think you could please come get me?"

"Lahni, what's going on there? What happened?"

"Well . . . nothing happened really. We got here and—and—his, uh—well, her name is Pat, and she wasn't supposed to be here when we got here, but she was and—"

"Oh, my God! Is she still there?"

"She's upstairs. But I'm sure she's leaving soon. It's just that I don't want to stay, and Dad said he'd drive me, but I don't want him to. I could take the train—"

"No, you can*not* take the train! I'm telling you now,

no matter what anybody else says, I'm your mother and *I* say you cannot take the train by yourself!"

"All right." I really hadn't meant to upset her. It made total sense that she was, but that's not what I had wanted. That's not why I'd called.

"Put your father on the phone."

"*Why*, Mom?" I didn't want them to fight. I definitely hadn't made the call so that they could have another fight. "Just tell me if you're coming, and I'll tell him, and that will be that."

There was silence for a moment. "Then tell him I'm coming. I'll be there as soon as I can."

"Okay." I was about to hang up when I heard her voice again.

"Lahni?"

"Yes, Mom?"

"Will you be all right?"

"I'll just wait for you, Mom, that's all."

I hung up the phone and turned in my father's direction. I could only imagine what it would have been like if I'd put him on the phone with my mother.

I walked over to where he was. "Well?" he asked me.

"She said she'll be here as soon as she can."

Just then the elevator doors opened, and there was Pat, dressed in a pink and white striped blouse and jeans. Her hair still wasn't completely dry, so it looked weird, like she'd put gel on part of it but missed other parts. She had on makeup. I suppose someone else would have thought she was attractive. I just thought how much younger she looked than my mother, although my mother looked more tired and old now than I'd ever seen before.

There was a row of big, leather-covered chairs next to where my father and I were standing. I went over to one of them and sat down, looking away from Pat and my father. Part of me wished they'd walk out the door together and disappear into the city. I'd wait until my mother picked me up and go back to New Clarion and try to pretend the whole day had never happened.

The two of them talked for a few minutes. I watched out of the corner of my eye. Then, exactly what I hoped wouldn't happen, did. She was coming over to me, by herself. My body stiffened; my jaw locked. *Don't,* I thought. Just *don't.*

"Lahni, I wanted to say I'm glad to have met you." She was standing in front of me. I could either be really rude and ignore her, or I could open my mouth and get it over with fast.

I looked up at her and forced the quickest fake smile possible. Then I looked back down into my lap, hoping she'd go away. She did.

My father came over right after that. "Do you want to go back upstairs now? You can wait there."

"No, thanks," I told him. "I'd like to stay here if it's okay."

"Lahni"—he leaned over so that maybe he couldn't be overheard—"you have an hour's wait, maybe more. You can't just sit here in the lobby."

I looked up at him. "Dad, I don't want to go upstairs, please. If I can't sit here, I can go outside."

He sat down in the chair next to mine and leaned over. "All right. All right. If you want to sit here, we'll sit here." I couldn't believe there wouldn't be more of a fight. My father always bragged how he had made this or that deal because he wasn't a quitter, because he never gave in. After a minute or two, he said, "Do you want to go get something to eat, at least? We could come right back here."

"No, thanks." Now I was wondering how we'd both be able to sit there without anything to say to each other, just waiting for my mother to arrive.

It wasn't easy. He sat looking straight ahead and so did I. One of the hotel people came up to him and asked if he was all right, and my father put on his business voice and said something silly about how his daughter had only been to the city a few times and really enjoyed sitting in the lobby. So that made *me* look like an idiot. But I didn't even care. I couldn't have been more angry with him no matter what he said about me. It didn't even surprise me that he used me as the excuse for us sitting there. I didn't think he was capable of accepting the blame for anything anymore. Anything bad that happened was a mistake, or somebody else's fault, or something he had no control over.

It might have been an hour, or it might have been seven. It certainly felt like closer to seven when my mother finally came through the doors of the Mayfair Hotel, looking like she'd run all the way from New Clarion. By that time, I was almost numb from sitting there, barely saying anything to my father, trying to imagine if we'd get along when we were all older.

My mother racing in was a bit of a shock. It wasn't that I'd forgotten why she was there. It was that I was calmer myself and didn't want her to make a big scene with my father. I just wanted to go home without talking about Pat anymore.

Right. Like that could actually happen. As she came toward us panting, my father and I jumped up from our seats.

"Hi, Mom," I said. She reached out and hugged me. Tightly.

Then she said to my father, "How could you be such a *jerk*!" I pulled away from her immediately. The last thing I wanted was for them to fight.

"Ursula—" my father started, but my mother cut him off.

"Don't! Because there's nothing you can say." This time she was much louder. If I'd thought people were staring at us before, we'd now become the Schuler Family Circus, except we were becoming less of a family by the second.

"What were you thinking? Huh? What were you thinking?"

"Mom," I pulled at her arm. "Please. Can we just go home?"

My mother stared at my father for what seemed like a very long time before she grabbed me and pushed me toward the hotel entrance.

As soon as we were outside, she blurted, "My God! What was he thinking!"

We kept walking with her shaking her head and squeezing me to her. When we got almost to the corner, she stopped suddenly. She was looking down the block and saying, "He can be stupid and careless with me, but not with you! Not with you!"

She started walking quickly, almost running. I realized then that she'd seen my father's car and was going toward it. What had started as loud talking had become shouting. "I won't allow it! I will not allow it!!"

When she got to his car, she went to the front and pulled at the windshield wiper. She twisted and turned it. "I will not allow it!" With both hands she was pulling the windshield wiper, and then she started kicking the car.

"Mom!" I called to her. I ran over to her and tried to make her stop. I grabbed her arm, but she wouldn't let go. "Mom, stop! You're going to get arrested. Please, stop!"

Of course, people were watching us. My mother was wild. I'd never seen her face all scrunched with her teeth bared like a wild dog. "I will not allow it! I will not allow it!"

I pulled her head toward me. We were nose to nose. "Stop it! Do you hear me? Mom, stop!"

She looked as if I'd called her from someplace she'd gone in a very short amount of time. And yet it had been very far away. She let go of the windshield wiper and backed away from the car. I grabbed her purse from the ground, put my arm around her waist, and pulled her even farther. A small circle of people had gathered around. They stood there watching us and talking about us as we went through them. An old woman said, "Somebody ought to call the police. Didn't anybody call the police?" I got very scared thinking that my mother could be arrested. I even wondered if I told them it was my father's car, what he'd do or say to them. It seemed to me, I was her only protection.

"Where's your car, Mommy?" I hadn't called her "Mommy" in years. But nothing sounded or felt too strange at that moment.

"It's down there," she said. She didn't point, so I didn't know where exactly she meant, and we just kept walking with our arms around each other. After a few minutes, I made myself look back. Some of the people were still standing there watching us, but there were no police. Not yet, anyway.

When we got to her car, I reached into her purse and took out her keys. "I don't think you should drive, Mom," I said.

She looked at me and held out her hand. She was still some other woman, not my mom. But whoever it was, said, "Don't worry. I'm all right. I am. I really am."

She took the keys and got into the car. I went around to the other side and got in beside her. "I am," she said again, looking straight ahead. And off we drove.

CHAPTER EIGHTEEN

Time was running out. Mr. Faringhelli was pressing me for which song I was singing in the competition, and I was supposed to ask Marcus, but I hadn't. I was more worried about Mom. Since we'd come back from New York, she was quieter than I'd ever seen her. There were times when I knew she was crying in her room, and there were times when I thought I saw that same look of fury I'd seen in New York. She apologized to me for what had happened with my father's car, but I'd told her I was sorry to upset her so much. We never heard anything about it from my father. At least if my mother did, she didn't tell me. But I couldn't think of it as "over." I could still picture her acting like someone I didn't know at all. I'd never seen her be more emotional than to tear up quietly at movies or at church. But the car thing? No way. Nothing close.

If I hadn't given my word to Mr. Faringhelli, I would have definitely dropped out of the competition. Except I hated when people went back on their word, so I was going to do what I'd said, even though I didn't care at all about singing, except in church. And I definitely was not in the mood for competing with anyone for anything.

I went to the next choir rehearsal determined to ask Marcus for his suggestion. I went up to him before the rehearsal, but he said, "Lahni, you'll have to ask me whatever it is later. We have got so much work to do tonight, and you will definitely be doing your share. So you better focus up, you hear?"

Before I even sat down, Marcus announced, "We are going to be doing a personal favorite of mine this Sunday, so y'all better be careful! Sing like you've never sung before! We're going to be doing "His Eye Is on the Sparrow" with Miss Carietta and Miss Lahni on the leads." Marcus winked at me. "See what I mean? You better focus up!"

I didn't have time to think about how I felt. But my hands were definitely shaking when he handed out the lyric sheets and mine had my name on it marked "soloist." We read the lyrics out loud, Carietta and I doing our parts alone. I thought the words were a little corny at first.

> "Why should I feel discouraged?
> Why should the shadows come?
> Why should my heart be lonely
> And long for heav'n and home?
> When Jesus is my portion
> My constant friend is He,
> His eye is on the sparrow,
> And I know he watches me.
> I sing because I'm happy
> I sing because I'm free
> His eye is on the sparrow
> And I know He watches me."

First, being new to church, I didn't know all that much about Jesus. I knew about God, and I understood that to some people Jesus was supposed to be God's son. But the whole thing about Jesus being my "portion" and a "constant friend" was a little hard for me to grasp. At first I thought I'd ask Marcus what the "portion" thing was all about, but then I decided if he thought it was a stupid question, he might change his mind about me doing the duet. As for the "constant friend" part, I couldn't make myself believe that *anybody* was *anybody's* constant friend—it wasn't real—and that was just the way it was.

That Sunday, before we sang it in church, I went over all the lyrics again carefully. I knew Marcus understood I wasn't exactly feeling the song like he always said we should. But he didn't want me to lose whatever confidence I had. The last time we rehearsed, he said to me, "It's gonna be all right, little sister. It's a little on the dry side, but it'll be fine. I know you'll come through." I knew what he meant by "dry." It was the last thing I wanted someone to say about my singing, but I'd done everything I could to understand what the song was about. I'd just have to act like Jesus *was* my constant friend *and* my portion. It was too late to do anything but pretend.

We all stood and Marcus started the intro. I began, trying to sound as sincere as I could. I wanted the words to fill me and move me like they did Carietta. But it wasn't happening. I tried a few of the tricks I'd learned to do with my voice, but they sounded like exactly what they were—tricks. I tried to imitate the sound that Carietta had, but with her standing right next to me, I felt like a fool as well as a fraud.

No matter how hard I tried, singing about being happy and free seemed absolutely ridiculous. And if Jesus, or even God, was always watching me, then they had to know nothing was going particularly well. So what good was their watching doing if all they were seeing was disaster?

Still, I got through my part. Carietta took over and, of course, people in the church shouted out "amen," and others, including my mother, wept. But I knew I'd failed. It was probably the last time Marcus would ask me to sing alone, and that was fine with me. If I had to sing stuff I didn't believe was true, then I shouldn't be singing at all.

After church I tried to avoid Marcus, but it didn't work. As he came toward me, I prepared myself to hear just how much I'd fouled up the duet. He said, "How you think you did today?"

"Lousy," I told him, trying to at least be honest about it.

Marcus laughed. "I'm not going that far. You should ease up on yourself a little. It's a song you got to grow into. When you do, you gonna *own* it." I couldn't believe he was letting me off so easily. I'd stunk and I knew it.

"In the meantime, though, don't get into the habit of mucking up what you do with tricks and imitation. If ya can't be nothin' else, be honest."

"Yes," I answered quietly. And then I felt ashamed. Bad was one thing, dishonest was another. And I'd been both. "I'm sorry, Marcus," I told him.

Marcus shook his head. "No need to be sorry. It's a waste of time. Like I said, one of these days you're gonna own that song. Maybe I'll be lucky enough to be in the room to hear it."

I watched him walk toward Carietta. They were going to their regular Sunday-afternoon-after-church meal. For Carietta, it could be a celebration. Once again, she'd sung from her heart and moved more than a hundred people.

I went out to the parking lot to meet my mother. All I could do was hope Marcus was right. Someday maybe I could sing a song like that and have it mean something real. How long that would be, I had no way of knowing.

I went to my coaching with Mr. Faringhelli the next day feeling like it was a waste of time, both his and mine. Next week was dress rehearsal and the week after that was the competition. I still hadn't made up my mind about what I was going to sing. Besides that, I knew now that there was a certain kind of singer I wanted to be that I wasn't. I knew I couldn't make people feel the kinds of emotions Carietta could, and I didn't think I'd change all that much anytime soon.

Mr. Faringhelli didn't exactly hide his impatience. "I thought you were serious about this, Lahni." The dark, wet circles under his armpits seemed to be bigger than ever. I knew that working with me was probably pretty stressful for him.

"I am serious about it, Mr. Faringhelli."

"Then how could you wait until the week before dress rehearsal and still not have a song chosen?"

I raised my head and leveled my voice, trying to sound surer of myself than I was. "Because it has to be *right*. It can't be just any song. I won't have a chance of winning if the song doesn't mean anything to me."

"Well," he sighed, with his hands on his hips, "you have a week. I don't see how you can have a chance of winning if you only have a week to work on the song after you've chosen it. But there's nothing else I can do to help you."

"I know, Mr. Faringhelli. Thank you." I started to pick up my backpack when he stopped me.

"Lahni, what do your parents think about this?"

I froze with my backpack halfway on. "Think about what?"

"Have you asked them to help you pick out a song? Do they know how little time you have left?"

"Yes, Mr. Faringhelli. They know."

The way he looked at me, I knew he was expecting more.

"They've decided to leave it up to me. They know they

can't pick something for me if it's not something I feel really strongly about."

"Yeah," he sighed again, with his hand at the back of his neck. "I guess you're right."

I continued to slowly pull on my backpack.

"It's just that I thought out of everyone in this, you would have been the most conscientious about preparing for it."

That stung. How could he accuse me of not preparing for the contest just because I didn't know which song I was singing? Didn't that mean exactly the opposite, that I cared enough to want the song to be exactly right? "I *have* prepared for it, Mr. Faringhelli," I told him. "In my own way."

I went down the hall half wishing he'd never been the one to second Katie's nomination. I didn't want to disappoint him any more than I wanted to lose the competition myself. Maybe I'd talk to Marcus again. Even if I wasn't as good as Carietta, there had to be something he thought I could sing decently. Except that I needed more than that. I needed something I had a chance of winning with. If only to thank Mr. Faringhelli for having faith in me.

CHAPTER NINETEEN

Go right back into school, go to the dean's office, and get Onyx 1, the wacko, thrown out of school! That's exactly what I thought to myself when I saw the photograph he'd taped to the seat of my bike.

It was face down, so I prayed nobody else had seen it. But I knew before I turned it over who it was from. I was just holding my breath that whatever the picture was wouldn't totally disgust me.

And there he was. In jeans, barefoot, without any shirt on. And a cap pulled down to the side. Grinning at me. Above his head there was a Magic Marker bubble. Inside the bubble it said, U R 4 ME.

I stood at the bike rack, holding the photograph, saying, "No, I'm not. I'm not for you. I'm not!"

. . .

It was two days later when I actually saw him again. I was in the locker room tying my sneakers, getting ready to go out onto the field for gym. Katie was already out there. She came running back into the locker room, screaming, "Lahni, come quick! You've got to see this! Hurry!"

I ran out behind her to the field. There was a pack of girls standing at the fence that separated Darby from Kent. When I got closer, I could see that they were watching two teachers from Kent leading two upper school black guys off the field. A few feet away, another teacher was standing next to Onyx 1, who had his head down, covering his nose and mouth with his hands. His fingers had blood all over them. His shirt was drenched. It looked like he'd been shot.

I ducked behind Katie, hoping he wouldn't look up and see me. Even though I was in the back of the group of girls watching, I was still nervous he'd somehow know I was there.

"What happened?" I whispered toward the back of Katie's head. Without turning, Katie answered, "I didn't get here until the end. But they had to drag those two guys off that imbecile who's been after you."

"Katie!" I snapped angrily. Was she trying to let everyone who didn't already know about Onyx 1 in on it?

"I'm sorry." She turned to me and lowered her voice. "From what I heard, the two guys were out here playing basketball, and Onyx what's-his-name kept trying to get them to let him play. When they refused, he started a fight with them. He called them—" Katie stopped. I could tell she didn't want to repeat whatever it was.

"Go on. Tell me!" I insisted.

Amber, who was standing next to Katie, piped up loudly, "He called them 'two black apes.'" She turned to watch for my reaction. "Over and over again—'you two black apes'!" I tried not to let the shock show.

"Which is when the two guys tried to beat the crap out of him," Katie added.

By now it was impossible for the conversation to be just between Katie and me. Chrissie leaned over and asked dramatically, "Did you see the knife?"

"What knife?" I asked.

"Your boy Onyx 1 had a knife." Of course, it would be Donna who'd call Onyx 1 "my boy." "Mr. Spiriotis just took it away from him. Look. You can still see it."

It was true. The teacher who was now handing Onyx 1 a handkerchief to stop his bleeding was holding an open pocketknife.

"Did he hurt them?" I asked.

"Them who? The black kids? No, he just kept bleeding

and waving around his little knife. Until the teachers came out and told the little boy to stop playing with his toy." How could Donna sound so disgusted with him? The last time I'd seen him, she was in the car with him, giggling like they were the best of friends. She'd delivered his note for him. How could she listen to herself turn on someone so fast without even offering some fake excuse?

We all watched the teacher take Onyx 1 by the arm and lead him inside. I couldn't help it. I started wondering if maybe he'd get thrown out of school and I'd never see or hear from him again.

By the time school was over, there were more details about what had happened at Kent. Supposedly, Onyx 1 had liquor on his breath. He wasn't thrown out of school, but he'd been suspended. For drinking, fighting, and carrying a knife. No one seemed to know for how long. I felt relieved. Onyx 1 was one less thing I had to worry about. At least for a while.

CHAPTER TWENTY

What I thought about mostly was my mom and how she was changing. It wouldn't have been hard to figure out if someone had asked me when it started. It started the day my father took the first suitcase of clothes to New York, and it got a lot more severe the day she came to pick me up from his hotel. It might not have been a drastic change to some people, but other than my father, I was the one who spent the most time with her. She had friends, a few, but not many. Before, it always seemed romantic to me that my father really was her best friend. I used to think that after him, came me. If that was true, she'd lost her best friend, and she was hardly speaking to the other one.

It wasn't that she meant to give me the silent treatment. I know it wasn't on purpose. She just seemed preoccupied most of the time, like she was going through the motions with me the best she could until she could be alone again. Even when she smiled, I felt it was because she was so good at being a mother, she could automatically do "good mother things," like make a smile look real and sound interested in whatever I was saying. But she wasn't really there. I knew it, and I was pretty sure she did too, except there wasn't much she could do about it.

The other thing I thought about was how close the competition was getting and I still didn't know what I was singing. The following Friday was dress rehearsal. I couldn't believe Mr. Faringhelli hadn't already thrown me out. Instead, what he actually told me was, "You think I'm going to make it easy for you, don't you? Have a screaming tantrum and tell you not to show up for dress rehearsal?" He shook his head. "Nope. I'm gonna keep on being a believer . . . even if it kills me."

The next Sunday in church, the first thing I did after saying hello to Marcus was to ask him what he thought I should sing for the competition. He said, "Little sister, I haven't had a chance to hear you sing a whole lot. But I would say, even though you've got to put in some time on "Sparrow," I'd go with that. It fits your voice nicely, and if you can sing it from your gut, you got a good chance of doin' somethin' with it."

"Doin' somethin' with it" was not exactly winning. But I'd asked him for a suggestion and he'd given it to me. "His Eye Is on the Sparrow." I wasn't sure. Of everything I'd sung since I started working toward the competition, it definitely hadn't wowed anyone. What kind of confidence booster was that? "You got a good chance of doin' somethin' with it." Well, thank you, Marcus. That ought to get me a first prize.

On Monday morning, I went straight to the fourth floor. The notice was posted on the Music and Art bulletin board.

Talent Competition in Two Weeks!

Talent Competition Dress Rehearsal This Coming Friday

Will begin promptly 7:30 p.m. The schedule is as follows:

7:30 Drama Club: Anne Seacrest

Faculty Mentor: Mrs. Lindsey

7:50 Music Department: Amber Merrill

8:10 Lahni Schuler

8:30 Lisa Shin

Faculty Mentor: Mr. Faringhelli

A wave of nervous dizziness went through me. Besides not knowing what I was going to sing, I also hadn't told either of my parents about the competition. Was I planning to show up and compete without them? What was I thinking I'd tell my mother next Friday night—*I'm going out for about an hour and a half. There's something going on at school, but it's totally trivial compared to what you already have on your mind?*

What I knew *could* be considered trivial was that I didn't have one thing in my closet that was right for a competition. I'd daydreamed about a few things I'd seen in magazines and one or two things that were my mother's, but I didn't own anything special enough to perform in. Usually my mother would have liked nothing better than an excuse to go shopping with me. I didn't nag her for the latest styles like other girls said they nagged their moms. Clothes didn't mean that much to me. And since I wore a uniform five days of the week, and a polyester choir robe covered my clothes on Sunday, wearing jeans and T-shirts the rest of the time felt like a vacation. But even fashion-moron-me knew I needed to do better than cutoffs and my father's old undershirt for next Friday night.

I sat in French class daydreaming I was Carietta singing in the competition, in front of the Darby girls and their parents. I was wearing the silver dress she'd had on the first time I met her and the backless shoes to match, with the toes as long and pointed as screwdrivers. I had her pony-tail, too, down to my waist. And the eyelashes. Just before I started, I smoothed my hair so everyone could see my

Stoplight Red nails with the squared tips. When I opened my mouth to sing the first few lines of a song *I* didn't even recognize, the judges all wrote my name at the top of their lists. No contest whatsoever. Carietta Lahni Schuler had won first prize. Partly for my stupendous looks and outfit but also for having a voice that was a combination of Mariah Carey's, Beyoncé's, and Fantasia's.

By the time French class was over, I decided I had to tell my mother about the competition for two reasons. The first one was I wanted her there, no matter how distracted or strangely she was acting. She wouldn't be that way always, and when it was over, I wanted her to remember that maybe I had made her proud. Whether I won or not. The second reason was I wanted to look nice for the competition and she was the one who could help me do that.

I would also let her know that it wasn't necessary to invite my father. I knew she'd feel awkward being in the same room with him, much less sitting together trying to pretend they were a happily married couple for my sake. I'd tell her I didn't want him there either. That would give her an excuse to agree not to tell him.

Donna Thoren couldn't wait to get it out. "Have you heard about that freak, Onyx 1?"

I sighed, remembering the days when Donna had practically ignored me. Now she felt perfectly comfortable stopping me in the hallway, so very sure I wanted to hear whatever she had to say.

"You mean that he was suspended? Yes, I heard."

"Lahni, you are so lame," she laughed. "That's last week's news. *This week's news* is that they only suspended him for three days. He'll be back at Kent on Thursday. Do you believe it?"

No. I couldn't. She was rattling on about how "they'd" decided it was too close to finals for Onyx 1 to be suspended for more than three days. I only half heard her. I kept picturing him with his hand over his face, his bloody shirt, and the teacher holding his knife. Why hadn't they expelled him? They said he had liquor on his breath and he'd pulled a knife on two boys. Why hadn't they thrown him out of school?

I walked away from Donna. I didn't want to hear any more of the details. They didn't matter. What mattered was that Onyx 1 was coming back to school in three days. And I'd just begun to think maybe he wouldn't be back at all.

CHAPTER TWENTY-ONE

You what? Why on earth didn't you tell me?"

"It's not as though we haven't had a lot going on around here, Mom. It wasn't as important as . . . everything else."

"Lahni, you're wrong. Pure and simple. It's more important. Because it's something you've achieved."

"I haven't achieved anything, Mom. I'm just *in* the competition. Even if I win, it doesn't mean I've achieved anything. It just means I sing better than two other girls. Plus Anne Seacrest who's not even singing. Big deal."

"Lahni, don't minimize this." My mother put her hands in front of her and looked up at the ceiling dramatically. "I mean it." She shook her head in disbelief. "Now, what are you singing?"

"I don't know."

"You don't *know*? You only have a week. And three days till the dress rehearsal. Didn't you say it was this Friday night?"

"And by Friday night, I'll know. For sure."

My mother shook her head again. She got up from the kitchen table. It was the first time we'd sat together there in days. Since my father was gone, the dining room was practically off-limits. Usually, when it was time to eat, she'd say she wasn't hungry. Or, if she did sit for a few minutes with me in the kitchen, she'd take a forkful of salad or a few sips of coffee and then get up and wander off. Tonight was a major exception. And I was glad I'd brought up the competition if only to have her really in the room with me for once.

"What are you wearing?"

I smiled and shrugged. I wasn't sure it would occur to her. "You mean for the competition?" I teased. "I don't know. I was thinking about borrowing something from Carietta at church. You should see some of the outfits she has on under her choir robe."

"Oh, you're just hysterical, Lahni. A laugh a minute. But I happen to be very serious. We have to go shopping. And soon."

"I know." I got up and started to help clear. "But I think it's going to be a big fat headache. You hate my taste, and I don't look good in anything you think I should wear."

My mother stopped scraping food into the trash. "Trust me. We are going to find something that you and I both will agree looks absolutely stunning, because it will." She put the plate on the sink and turned to me. "It's not as though you're not attractive, Lahni. You realize what a pretty girl you are, don't you?"

"I think I'm all right." I would rather not have had that conversation, though. All it seemed to do was make me feel uncomfortable.

"You are more than 'all right.' You've got a great little figure. Good legs—"

"Mom, *please.*"

"Okay, okay. But you should know, Lahni. It doesn't hurt to know what you look like."

"All right." I wanted her to stop. If she'd started to talk about boys, I'd start thinking about Onyx 1. And if I started to think about Onyx 1, my whole night would be ruined. If a boy was going to like me, I thought, why did it have to be him? If I was such a "pretty girl," why was the one boy who was sending me pictures of himself a wacko at Kent who tried to act like he was black but called black boys "apes"?

Thursday I had my last coaching with Mr. Faringhelli before the dress rehearsal. As soon as I walked in, he said, "So what I'm looking for in your hands is a piece of sheet music. And if I don't see one, it means you're about to pull it out of your backpack, is that right?"

"No," I said, "but I definitely know what I'm going to sing."

He put a paper cup of coffee on the piano and clapped his hands. "Finally, finally, finally! What is it?"

"Do you know a song called 'His Eye Is on the Sparrow'?"

"Of course I do." Mr. Faringhelli sat at the piano and immediately started the opening chords. It didn't sound at all like how Marcus played it, though.

I smiled. "That's what I'm doing for the competition."

Mr. Faringhelli stretched back on the piano bench, grinning. "Could you please tell me why it was such a big secret?"

"It wasn't. Really. I just wasn't sure before, that's all."

"Well, I think it's a great choice for you. Have you been working on it?"

"I sang it with this choir I'm in." I wasn't going to tell him about the duet with Carietta, considering it hadn't gone that well.

"Excellent. Then I hope you have the sheet music cause you're going to need it tomorrow. I mean I kind of know it, but if I'm going to play for you, I definitely need the sheet music."

"I'll have it tomorrow."

He stood up from the piano and laughed. "Am I relieved! I didn't know *what* you were going to do!"

I felt so good knowing he understood I wasn't going to let him down. I picked up my backpack. Then I thought of something. "Mr. Faringhelli?"

"Yes, ma'am?"

"What did you mean when you said, 'If I'm going to play for you'? Aren't you going to play for all of us?"

"No. As a matter of fact, I'm not. Lisa's father plays the violin. She asked if it was all right for him to accompany her, and I said it would be fine. Why? Is there somebody you'd like to play for you?"

I hesitated for a minute. "No. I mean, I'm not sure."

Mr. Faringhelli rolled his eyes. "Lahni Schuler, there you go again. Trying to make a basket case out of me. Will you know by tomorrow?"

I had already gone somewhere else in my mind. "Yes . . . sure . . . definitely. I'll know by tomorrow."

I left his room singing under my breath. I knew what I had to do, if I could only get up the nerve.

Katie and I left the building together. I'd told her about the incident with Onyx 1 and the photograph, and from then on she was always asking when I was leaving school so we could ride home together. Still, going to the bike rack, knowing he'd been allowed back in school, I held my breath and prayed that all that would be there would be my bike, with nothing attached to it.

"Are you nervous about tomorrow night?" Katie asked.

I was so relieved to see no pictures or messages—nothing but my bike. "No," I answered her. "Well, a little."

As soon as we turned onto the main road, I picked up speed. Katie called out to me, "Lahni, where are you going? You're flying down the road like you've got a big date or something!"

"I do!" I called back.

"Yeah, right!" she yelled. I rode faster.

We stopped at our turnoff to say good-bye. Her face was flush from trying to keep up with me. "Are you serious? Do you really have a date?"

I looked at her face and realized how much she was hoping I'd say yes. Katie talked about having a date like it was what she wanted as much as anything and also like she thought she'd be thirty before it happened. If it could happen for me, I bet she was thinking, then maybe it could happen for her.

"I do," I told her. "I do have a date."

"Who? How come you didn't tell me?"

I laughed. "Because I just decided I'd have it."

Katie looked puzzled and anxious for an explanation. "Who is it? Tell me!"

I got on my bike and started to pedal away, calling over my shoulder, "Don't worry. You'll meet him."

And I thought to myself, *At least, I hope you will.*

CHAPTER TWENTY-TWO

Marcus usually got to rehearsal before anyone else, but on Thursday evening I got there first. The church custodian let me in, and I went to the piano and waited.

When he came in, I called to him, "Hi, Marcus." He walked over to me. Marcus had so many different smells going on, his coming into the room was like going into the men's cologne department at a department store that also sold perfumed hair products and scented candles in the same area.

"Hey, what you know, little sister? You're here mighty early." He put his overstuffed briefcase down on the floor and took off his suit jacket. Even in May Marcus wore a suit, not only to church on Sunday but to choir practice every Thursday evening. Usually under the jacket was a shirt that you'd never see on anyone—man or woman—except Marcus.

The first hour he would take off his suit jacket, fold it neatly, and put it over the back of one of the metal folding chairs. The second hour he would open his shirt, and the jeweled cross would dangle in the air over the keys and hit them as he played. He always had a handkerchief that he kept for wiping his round, damp face. He'd take it out of his jacket pocket at the beginning of rehearsal, set it on top of the piano on a pile of music, and put it back in his pocket at the end.

Marcus reached for one of the folding chairs and laid his jacket across the back of it.

I told him, "I got here early because I wanted to ask you something."

Marcus took his handkerchief out of his jacket pocket and patted the perspiration on his forehead and cheeks and under his chin. Then he placed the handkerchief on top of the piano. "Yes? What's that?"

"You know the competition at school I told you about?"

"How am I gonna forget that? It's important, isn't it?"

I was suddenly very embarrassed. I knew he was trying to be kind. What would make a Darby School talent competition important to Marcus Delacroix III, even if a girl in his choir was in it?

"Well, I would like to make my mother proud of me,

at least. She could use something good to happen right about now."

Marcus ran his hand over the piano top very slowly. He looked like a blind man, getting to know what it felt like for the first time.

"You know, I've never been introduced to your mom. But I think I know who she is."

I hadn't even thought about introducing the two of them to each other. I wondered if Marcus thought I was embarrassed to because she was white.

"I will, Marcus. I never thought about it. But I want you to meet her. I do."

Marcus smiled. "I don't think I've ever seen your dad, though."

"He doesn't go to church. None of us did before my mom and I came here." I usually got so angry when people asked me about things I considered private, but I didn't mind Marcus asking me at all.

"Is your father coming to your competition?"

"I dunno. I haven't told him about it yet."

Marcus picked up his handkerchief again and delicately patted each side of his nose. "I see."

"Marcus," I said, trying to make it sound like I didn't feel any particular way about it, "my parents are getting a divorce."

"Oh." Marcus put the handkerchief back down on the piano. He looked at me and cocked his head to the side like a bird.

"That's all right. You and your mom will do fine. Me and my mom did."

"Your parents were divorced too?"

Marcus laughed. "No, lil sister. My father was G.B.I.S.—Gone Before It Started. Never saw him. Never even saw a picture of him till I was about eight, and I had to find that on my own. After awhile, it didn't matter. I didn't want to see him. But everybody's different. You'll be okay. Better than okay. You'll see."

He reached down and opened the piano. His fingers skittered up and down the keys. "You're gonna wake up girl, tomorrow mornin'," he sang in a high voice, "you're gonna wake up girl and see, anything that ain't holdin' you down, is helpin' you to be freeeee!"

I smiled.

"Now, what were you gonna ask me about your competition?"

I was suddenly nervous again. "It's next Friday night. And the dress rehearsal is tomorrow. At six thirty."

"Whoooaaa! It's right up on us, isn't it? You planning to make an announcement to the choir tonight?"

"No. I mean, I hadn't planned to."

"Well, why not? You got some fans in this group. You better let your fans know what you're doing. I don't want them gettin' on me, talkin' about 'why didn't you tell us?'"

"Okay," I said quietly, but I didn't think I really could stand up in front of a group of adults who were still mostly strangers and ask them to come to hear me sing at a middle school talent competition.

"Marcus, the reason I got here early was to ask you . . . I thought the music teacher was accompanying all of us, but he told me yesterday that I could ask anyone I wanted to, and . . . I wanted to know if you would consider playing for me tomorrow and next Friday." Even with everything else we'd talked about, I could barely believe I'd gotten it out. But I had and now the worst he could say was no.

Other people from the choir had started to trickle in. All of them called out a hello to Marcus and me, and both of us greeted them. I stood about a foot away from him, waiting as patiently as I could. Carietta came in. "I called you, but you had already left," she told Marcus.

"What did you want?" Marcus asked.

"To tell you I was in the mood for some Chinese food tonight, so that's where we're going after rehearsal. Don't give me no argument." They both laughed heartily.

"How you doin' tonight, Miss Lahni?" Carietta leaned over and gave me a kiss on the cheek. I kissed her back.

Marcus picked his handkerchief up off the piano top again and wiped his forehead and patted his cheeks and under his chin. He slid his dark glasses down to the end of his nose so you could see his eyes. He cleared his throat and said loudly to the whole room, "Lahni here is in a school talent competition next Friday night. Y'all should go on out and support her. She's a good member of this choir, and we know she's got a voice."

Everyone in the room applauded. Carietta put her arm around me. The mix of smells between the two of them was enough to make you faint. Especially if you were already feeling as lightheaded as I was.

Marcus said, "I'm gonna be there because I'm gonna be playin' for her." And I started to applaud too. "Thank you," I said looking up at him. "Thank you, Marcus."

He leaned down and played something jazzy. "We're gonna be fine, lil sister."

He laughed. "You watch what I tell ya."

CHAPTER TWENTY-THREE

Friday morning I went to the notice board in the music and art department just to see if anything had changed. I was glad I did. Anne Seacrest's name from the Drama Club was crossed out. Apparently, she wasn't in the competition anymore. The schedule of rehearsals had been changed. Amber's new time was seven thirty, and I'd been moved up to seven fifty. I went to Mr. Faringhelli's room not expecting him to be there, but he was, coffee cup in hand.

"I just saw the board. What happened to Anne Seacrest?"

He took a sip of coffee. "And good morning to you, too, young lady."

"I'm sorry," I said.

"Just kidding," he said, and smiled. "I don't know what happened. I imagine she's dropped out for some reason or another. I was told to adjust the schedule now that it's just the music department involved, so I did. We're giving special prizes to art students, but it's just you three who are performing. And maybe the Darby orchestra to fill out the evening. Are you ready for tonight?'

I knew I was beaming. "Yep. I have an accompanist. His name is Marcus Delacroix III."

Mr. Faringhelli took another sip of coffee. "Well, you go, Lahni Schuler." It always embarrassed me when teachers used kids' expressions, even Mr. Faringhelli who could have gotten away with it better than most. "Make sure you tell him your time has changed."

"Oh! You're right! I have to do that!" I turned to run out of the room, then turned back. "See you tonight, Mr. Faringhelli."

He waved sleepily as he took another sip.

Several times I called Marcus to tell him that our rehearsal time had changed, but I couldn't reach him. Finally I left a message on his voice mail, repeating the directions to Darby and telling him the new time.

Every time Katie asked about the date I'd had the night before, I'd pretend I was too nervous to say anything, in case I was overheard. By the time school was over, I thought she'd burst at the seams if she didn't get an answer.

"Are you gonna tell me or not?" she asked at the bike rack.

"Tell you what?" I teased.

"Okay. Fine. Don't tell me," she said, pouting.

"Oh, that! Katie, I told you, you'll meet him. Don't you believe me?"

"Yes, I believe you, but why can't you tell me who he is? Why does it have to be a surprise? Can't you even tell me his initials?"

"Katie!" I looked at her like parents look at children who are bugging them out and the parents are trying not to lose their patience. We got on our bikes in silence. I almost felt bad about teasing her. Even if she knew it was Marcus I'd been talking about the day before, she wouldn't understand how nervous I had been to ask him to accompany me and how I still couldn't quite believe he'd said yes.

At our turnoff, Katie pulled up next to me and asked, "Do you want me to come to rehearsal tonight?"

"Why would you want to do that?" I really didn't have a clue.

Katie looked hurt. "I thought I'd just come in case you needed anything."

"Oh. I think I'll be okay. You definitely plan to be there for the real thing next week, don't you?"

Katie brightened. "Are you kidding? Of course!" After a second she said, "Will this guy be there?"

I smiled, trying to look mysterious. "I'm pretty sure. He said he would be."

"Wow." Katie looked like I'd announced my engagement. Maybe she really would be disappointed when she found out it was Marcus I was talking about. Oh, well. I didn't care. He was absolutely my favorite man in the world right now. And as far as I was concerned, I could hardly wait until our next date, which was only a few hours away.

I was hoping there'd be a message when I got home, saying that Marcus knew about the new rehearsal schedule, but there wasn't. If he came late, I wasn't sure what Mr. Faringhelli would do. I didn't have the sheet music for anyone else to play, so I wouldn't be able to sing unless Marcus was there.

My rehearsal time was 7:50, but I still wanted to be early to calm my nerves. I asked my mother to drop me off at seven thirty. That way, maybe I could get a chance to see Mr. Faringhelli. I could explain about Marcus before Amber went in for her rehearsal. If Marcus came on time, fine, but if he didn't, Mr. Faringhelli wouldn't be surprised if I couldn't go in.

As I got out of the car, my mom asked, "Do you want me to wait until you hear what your teacher has to say?"

"No, mom. Mr. Faringhelli is cool. If I have to be last, I have to be last. I'll just wait, that's all."

"Well, come here, then," she said and reached out her arms. I went to her side of the car and hugged her through the open window. "I love you, honey bunny." She'd tucked me in when I was little saying that, but she only said it now when she was very emotional. I knew how much she wanted me to do well in this competition.

"Love you too, Mom," I said, and pulled away gently. My mother's moods were so unpredictable since my father left. If I stopped too long to think about it, I wouldn't be able to concentrate on what I had to do.

I stepped away from the car.

"Lahni."

"Yes, Mom?"

She pointed at my feet. "Beyoncé does *not* sing with her sneakers untied."

I looked down, nodded, and rolled my eyes. "Mom, *please*."

She beeped the horn in a funny rhythm—ba-ba ba ba—ba ba!—and laughed. Then she drove slowly out of the parking lot, honking good-luck as she went around to the front and down the Darby entrance road.

I bent to tie my sneakers when I heard Mr. Faringhelli calling me. He was standing at the back entrance of school. It was the easiest way to get into the auditorium, especially from the parking lot. Mr. Faringhelli had his usual paper cup of coffee. "Why are you so early?" he called to me. "Are you having a case of nerves? You're not due until almost eight."

"I know, Mr. Faringhelli, but I couldn't get in touch with my accompanist, Marcus. I mean, I left a message, but I'm not sure he got it. I wanted to be here early to tell you, and if I have to wait until Lisa finishes, I will."

"Shoot. They're in there still hanging lights, for Pete's sake, and Amber is not even here yet. And she's supposed to be first."

"I know." I couldn't help smiling at the fact that Amber was late. Everyone in school probably thought she was going to win, including her. But according to Katie, she'd missed almost all the coachings and bragged that she didn't need them anyway. "I've been singing since I was three," Katie claimed she'd heard her say. "Nicky just wants to get me alone in his room." I wasn't as disgusted at what she'd said as Katie was, but maybe that was because Katie's imitation of her was so funny.

Mr. Faringhelli took a last swallow and tossed the cup into a metal trash basket. "You may as well relax," he told me. "We can't start until they finish hanging, and even then we can't start until Amber gets here."

"Okay," I said. He went inside to the auditorium. I sat on the curb in the parking lot.

About ten minutes later, Amber's father drove up and dropped her off. She bounced over and asked, looking down at me sitting there, "Why are you out here? Hasn't it started yet?"

"Mr. Faringhelli's inside with the custodians. They're fixing the lights. But since you're first, they'll probably start when you go in."

She seemed to ignore the suggestion that they'd begin as soon as she showed her face. "Isn't this soooo much fun? I can't wait until next Friday. Do you know what you're going to wear?"

"No, not yet," I mumbled. I glanced behind me at the auditorium to give her another clue.

"I just got the most gorgeous dress. It is just soooo gorgeous."

I took a deep breath. If I'd had a cell phone, I could have tried Marcus right then instead of having to listen to Amber. "Mr. Faringhelli was looking for you. I told him if I saw you, I'd tell you to go on in."

"Oh. Well, I guess I should then." Amber tossed her hair back over her shoulders and pulled at her tank top, which was cut off so high it looked like an old bra that had lost its shape. "This song I picked is so hard," she whined. "I can't believe I picked such a hard song. Mr. Faringhelli loooves it, but it is sooooo hard."

I tried my best to look sympathetic, thinking it would encourage her to keep going through the doors into the auditorium.

"Is *your* song hard?" she cooed.

I'd had it. I started to dig my fingers into my sneakers, fidgeting with my ankles and the bottoms of my feet. "It's, it's, I don't know, not so hard I guess."

It seemed as though she had yet another foolish remark to offer when I said, "You should prob'ly go in. They're waiting for you."

Amber looked slightly insulted. "Okay, I'm going," she huffed. She pulled open the glass door. "See ya," she said, and I turned and smiled over my shoulder.

I jumped to my feet as soon as she was inside and crossed my eyes. *Oh, she's annoying.* I wished Katie had been there so she could do another wicked imitation of her.

I walked out a few feet into the parking lot. "Please Marcus, please." At this point, I was anxious to go in, sing, and get it over with.

I walked farther out, beginning to hum my song. I

stepped up onto one of the little concrete islands that the parking lot lights were on. I stood under the light, pretending it was shining down on me. I patted my hair gently and smoothed my gown. I nodded to Marcus in his tuxedo that I was ready and he raised his hand to the orchestra to let them know. I closed my eyes, listening to the sixty violins playing my introduction. Then I began. *I sing because I'm happy. I sing because I'm free . . . Oh, his eye is on—*

"Yo." I opened my eyes. It was Onyx 1. He was wearing a gray basketball shirt and the red and black striped ski cap pulled down so that I could only see a fringe of his hair. I looked at his mouth and the scar under his bottom lip. "I thought tonight was the show." Even though I thought I knew what he sounded like, I couldn't have because I'd never heard him actually speak before.

"It's the rehearsal. The show is not until next week." I tried to sound like it was a perfectly normal conversation and I wasn't nervous and I definitely wasn't scared.

"You're in it, right?" Of course, he knew I was. That's why he was there, wasn't it?

"Yes."

I thought about the fight with the two boys and the knife he'd had. My heart jumped. He smiled.

"Little Miss Lahni."

Hearing him say my name made my skin crawl. I stared at him. Why, even when I thought about the knife, didn't I turn around and run? Why was I still standing there?

"What do you want?" I asked him.

He looked surprised, as though he hadn't expected to have to do anything but stand there trying to look tough.

"You wanna go out with me sometime?"

When he said it, all I could think about was that I wished Katie could have heard him. As desperate as she was to have some boy ask her what he'd just asked me, how would she like to be here where I was now, finally having the chance to say yes?

"No," I told him.

"Why? I betcha you never been out with anyone before."

"Doesn't matter. I don't want to go out with *you*." I backed around the parking light post behind me, but I missed the step down. I stumbled backward. I tried to catch myself, but I fell. I froze, looking up at Onyx 1. He was sneering at me. He took a quick step forward so that he was practically standing over me. I sat there on the concrete glaring up at him.

"I heard you weren't a hundred percent black girl. I just wanted to see for myself."

I bit my bottom lip hard. Suddenly, I didn't care how scared I might have been of him before. When he said that to me, I wanted to jump up and punch him. I didn't think about him being dangerous. All I could see was the sneer and a white boy standing over me telling me he wanted to see how black I was.

"How would you know?" I shouted at him, scrambling to my feet. "How would you know if I was a hundred percent black? You wanna see who I am? You come near me, you follow me, you send me another note." By this time, without realizing it, I was so close to him, I could see his right eye twitching. I pointed my finger toward his face. If he thought he was going to hurt me now, I was daring him to try it. "They may not have put you in jail for pulling a knife on those two boys, but you keep messing with me! I'll show you what I am!" I didn't even know what I was threatening. All I knew was that my head was flipping from side to side and my eyes were wide with anger and my arms were ready to knock him to the same place I'd just gotten up from.

Onyx 1 stared at me as though I was possessed. And I was. Before I could think about it, I put all my weight on one hip with my legs spread apart like I was ready to rumble. The same voice that wasn't mine even though it was coming from me said, "*Now* what do you have to say,

Onyx 1?" And I said his name like it was the silliest thing I'd ever heard attached to somebody.

He just kept staring.

Whoever it was that had taken over my body gave him this look of disgust that said, "Uh-huh. Nothing. That's what I thought." Then I turned very slowly away from him and walked toward school, swinging my hips like I didn't even know they could move. When I got nearer to the auditorium door, I stopped. I knew he wasn't behind me. I was safe.

At first, I heard nothing. Then I heard a car door slam and a few seconds after that, a motor start. By the time I got to the back entrance of school, I could hear him driving out of the parking lot. I made sure not to turn my head, but out of the corner of my eye I saw him just as he went around the building. No music. No noise. Gone.

Oh Lahni, I thought. *Who in the world was that? Who was that girl that made Onyx 1 get in his car and drive away?* I stopped and planted my feet just like she had. "Now what do you have to say?" I growled, imitating her. "Uh-huh. Nothing. That's what I thought." And I shook my head. *Who was she Lahni? Who was that girl?*

Less than a minute later, Marcus was pulling up toward me. Their cars must've passed each other.

Marcus got out of his car, took out his handkerchief,

and wiped his forehead. "Whooo! Got your message, Miss Lahni. Got here soon as I could."

"We should go right in," I told him. "I'm so glad you're here." I grabbed his arm without thinking about it, but when I realized I'd done it, I didn't let go.

"So I made it on time, little sister?" Marcus laughed. I'm sure he was surprised that I was holding on to him.

"Oh, absolutely," I answered. "You definitely made it on time!"

CHAPTER TWENTY-FOUR

"I don't know exactly what happened in there, but we got to do better than we did if we gonna win a competition."

"I know it wasn't very good. I'm sorry."

Marcus and I stood outside the auditorium. My mom was waiting anxiously in the car to hear how it had gone. She must have sensed something watching us standing there, both looking glum.

"Don't apologize to me," Marcus said. "You got to figure out for yourself what that was all about. I mean, I know we haven't done it together since you sang it at church, but I don't think that was the problem. It seemed like your nerves got the better of you."

I thought he was right. Not my nerves about singing the song. No, I think I was still shaking from the conversation I'd had just before we went inside, the conversation with Onyx 1. My nervousness had shocked me, too. After I'd sung, I tried to make sense of it.

Every time we sang at church, Marcus told us to "focus up," which meant to calm ourselves down and concentrate on what we were there to do. I definitely hadn't done that before I sang at the dress rehearsal. I'd left Onyx 1 and run inside with Marcus just as Amber was coming out. We got into the auditorium, I introduced Marcus to Mr. Faringhelli, and then I sang. Somewhere in the middle of the song, I realized most of me was still outside trying to make sure Onyx 1 would leave me alone for good. And whatever I thought I was doing with Marcus on our song stunk.

"There wasn't any audience to speak of, so that couldn't have been the problem. There was just your teacher, Mr. Farinwhatever, who seems to really think you have talent, and those two or three men working on the lights and the sound. You sang it in front of a hundred people before and sounded three times as good." Marcus shook his head. "No, you got to figure out what happened in there for sure."

"I really am sorry, Marcus. It was my nerves. I know it was. But I promise I'll be better next Friday night. I promise."

"Oh no!" Marcus stomped his foot lightly. "You got to do better than 'better'! I want brilliance next Friday night.

Do you hear me, Miss Lahni Schuler? *Brill eeeee uuunce!"*

"Yes, sir. You'll have it." I smiled through my embarrassment. I was sorry to have let him down, and myself as well. All I could do was work harder. At least I was pretty sure I wouldn't be having any more conversations with Onyx 1 before next Friday night. That would make a difference for sure.

"Well? How did it go?" my mother asked when I opened the car door. " I was thinking I'd get out and introduce myself to Marcus, but it didn't seem like a good time. Didn't you have a good rehearsal?"

"It was pretty awful, actually." I couldn't lie.

"Nooooo." My mother looked at me in shock. "How could that be true? I've heard you sing that song. And Marcus was playing for you. How could it be awful?"

"Mom, would it be possible for us not to talk about it right now?" I didn't want to shut her out. I would have liked nothing better than to tell her every detail, but I needed the safety of the car just then and a ride home without having to say anything to anyone.

Once we were home, though, I asked my mother, "Do you have a few minutes to talk about something?"

"Of course, Lahni. Honey, what is it? Let's go in here." She backed into the kitchen, watching me instead of where she was going. Her face was full of alarm. It wasn't really how I wanted to begin.

"Mom, I think I know why I had such a horrible rehearsal."

She sat across from me at the kitchen table, wide-eyed.

"You see, a while ago, this boy who goes to Kent who calls himself Onyx 1 . . ."

That's how my explanation of the whole evening started. I told her everything, from the very beginning right through "and then Marcus drove up and we went in, and before I knew it, I was onstage singing."

As soon as I stopped talking, my mother was on her feet. I recognized the expression on her face immediately. It was the same one she'd had when she came out of the hotel in New York and went crazy on my father's windshield wipers.

"I'm going to have him arrested." She put both hands on her hips and then slammed one hand down on a counter. "They should have put him away when he pulled a knife on those two boys. But now he will be." She started out of the kitchen.

"Mom! Wait! What are you doing? Where are you going?" I ran behind her into my father's study.

"I'm going to call Dean Surloff and tell her what you told me. You understand someone needs to put a stop to this kid, don't you?"

"Mom, please. Could you listen for a minute?"

She whirled around and faced me. "I only wish I'd known sooner. You wouldn't have had to go through *half* of this." She picked up her personal phone book and started looking for Dean Surloff's number.

"Mom, I don't want you to call anyone. I want you to leave it alone. I only told you because . . ." And I had to stop and think why I really did tell her. I went very slowly, putting it together for myself as I spoke. "I wanted to tell you because I was hoping you would think I did the right thing. I didn't want to be scared anymore, and I thought you'd be proud of me for doing something about it."

"But you didn't have to let it get this far." Now she sounded angry. That wasn't what I'd wanted at all.

I tried to speak to her like she spoke to me when she hadn't meant to make me angry. "Mom, I'm not afraid of him anymore. If he was going to do anything to me, he had his chance already."

"That doesn't mean he won't try some other time," my mother said. "It's clear he's disturbed, and he's already been violent. Lahni, I don't want to take any chances."

"Mom, I know you have to be concerned because you're my mother, but could you please let me be a part of the decision this time. Please."

She stopped going through her phone book. "Do you

seriously want me to listen to you tell me how this boy who has already tried to hurt two other people and has harassed you, followed you in his car, and waited for you in an empty parking lot on the school premises—you want me to listen to this and agree to do nothing about it? What kind of a parent do you think I'd be?"

"If you would just sit down for a minute so you could listen to me, I'll tell you."

My mother paused for a second, then sat down in my father's desk chair and looked up at me. That made me feel uncomfortable so I sat on the small sofa opposite her.

I took a breath and began. "I have to get through this competition. And I really want to do well. Just like I couldn't concentrate today because I was thinking about Onyx 1 before I went in and sang, it will be the same thing if you start to make trouble for him now. It will be a big mess and I won't be able to think about anything else. I just want to get through the competition and finish the year in peace."

"Frankly, I don't care about making trouble for him. I'm trying to protect you so you *can* finish the year in peace. I think he's already gotten *himself* into trouble."

I pulled closer to her and kept my voice very low. "No matter what he did before, when he finally asked me if I wanted to go out with him, I said no. He didn't pull a knife and he didn't yell or call me names. He just stood there looking like it wasn't at all what he expected to happen, and I wasn't the Lahni Schuler he thought I'd be. So now it's over. Can we please leave him alone?"

"But from what you said about this boy, you could still be in danger!"

"Mom, I'm not stupid. I'd know if I were in danger. And I'd tell you. But I know I'm not."

She looked at me, then she asked very quietly, "Are you telling me everything that happened?"

At first, I was angry, feeling like she thought I was a liar. But then I knew the only way I might get what I wanted was to make sure she knew I was telling the truth.

"Yes. I told you everything."

"You know, even if I agree to not report this to someone, your father never will."

"Mom! You can't tell him!"

My mother stood and tossed her phone book on the desk. "How can I not tell your father? How can I know something this serious has happened to you and agree not to tell your father? Lahni, now you're asking too much!"

"But if you tell him, it'll be exactly like you said—he won't care what I want; he'll try to have Onyx 1 arrested or at least thrown out of school permanently. It will be what *he* wants to do, not what I want. But I'll be in the middle of it. Not you and not him. Me!"

She put her hands up to her face and pulled at her hair. "Ugh! You are asking the impossible!"

I stood up and hugged her tightly. "I promise, if I didn't think I was safe, I'd tell you."

"I'd never forgive myself, Lahni—"

"It'll be all right. I swear it will."

She unwrapped my arms from around her waist and held my face in her hands. "I want you to know I can't make *you* any promises, Lahni. If something happens and I think I need to protect you, I will. Even if you don't think I should."

She pulled me to her again. I remembered being in the parking lot. I remembered being afraid when I first saw Onyx 1 but making the decision not to run from him.

"Mom?"

"Yes, hon?"

"Why do you think he's so . . . confused in the way that he is?"

"Oh, Lahni, why would you want to concern yourself with why that boy is confused? As long as his confusion doesn't affect my daughter, I'm perfectly content to let that be his parents' problem."

"But it's the whole black-and-white thing. He calls himself a word that means 'black,' he thinks he likes me because I'm black, but then there's the fight with the two black guys and he calls them apes because they won't let him into their game. What's his problem?"

My mother sighed and sat down on the sofa. "I guess you used the right word. 'Confused.' I don't know the boy or where he comes from or who his parents are. But there are lots of people who are confused about who they are and what they are. And they get angry about it. Confusion can make you pretty angry, I think, especially when you're young."

She took my hand and pulled me down next to her. "What's important to me is that you aren't confused. About who you are."

"I'm not," I said, feeling embarrassed.

"No, I'm serious, Lahni. No matter what happens with your father and me, neither one of us wants you to be confused about who you are. I certainly don't. I have a beautiful, African American daughter whom I love and want to keep safe. That's who you are to me, and a lot more. But I'm not confused about loving you, and I don't want you to think that I don't know who my daughter is, because I do."

"I know," I told her.

When I looked at her, her eyes were red and wet. One tear was about to fall. I looked away on purpose before it did. I held my mother instead and whispered, "Thank you."

CHAPTER TWENTY-FIVE

Before I went to bed that night, Mom came into my room. "I can't get our conversation out of my mind, Lahni."

Oh no, I thought. I don't have any more arguments left.

"I'll go along with keeping what happened with that Onyx character between us, but you have to tell your father about the talent competition. You have to invite him. And soon."

I sighed. "All right. If that's what you want. I didn't think you'd care if he came or not."

"He's your father. You can't avoid telling him about what's important in your life because of what's going on between the two of us. He'd be very hurt, and he'd also hold me responsible."

"All right, Mom, I'll tell him."

• • •

I knew when I called on Saturday morning that it wouldn't be an easy conversation. "Talent competition? Why didn't you tell me before now?" he barked. "I'm sure you've known about it for months. I'm sure your mother knew about it too."

"Dad," I tried to explain lamely, "I wasn't sure if I was really going to be in it. I kept going back and forth about it. Then I couldn't decide on a song. I didn't want you to come if I was going to be embarrassing." All reasons I thought would appeal to him.

"But it's literally *days* away. I can't believe that you just decided *days* ago and they still let you be a part of it. I just don't believe it."

"I'm sorry, Dad. I know it's short notice. But I really do want you to come. If you want to think about it and let me know . . ." I wanted to hang up. Either he was going to come or he wasn't. You'd think he'd want to make it up to me, considering the last time I'd spoken to him was in his hotel lobby after we'd surprised his girlfriend. I wondered if she was with him now.

"I don't have to think about it, Lahni. Of course I'm coming. I'm your father. I should be there."

It sounded like when he bragged to my mother and me about closing a deal. He always told us, "You end by restating your position firmly. Then you tell them the details will be forwarded in writing and you hang up before they change their minds." There weren't any details to be forwarded, so I supposed now he would hang up, knowing I couldn't change my mind.

"What time did you say this thing is?"

"It's at seven thirty. On Friday."

"I don't suppose I'll get a chance to see you beforehand." There was silence. What could I say? It's not as though we'd all be at home getting ready together. No, he probably wouldn't see me before the competition, unless we made an appointment.

"No, Dad, I guess not."

"Then I suppose I'll have to call you on Thursday night to wish you good luck. Will you be around?" It was such an awkward conversation about seeing each other. I wondered if this was the way it would always be.

I knew I had choir practice on Thursday, but he didn't know about choir and this was definitely not the time to bring it up.

"I have rehearsal, I think. At school. But I'll be home at about nine thirty."

"Well," I heard him sigh, "I'll try to reach you after nine thirty or so."

"Sure, that should be okay."

"All right. Bye, Lahni."

"Bye, Dad."

So it didn't end the way he said his deal closings did. It didn't sound like either one of us was all that pleased with the way the conversation had ended. But I'd done what my mom asked me to and now my father was coming. Was I glad? Considering what a creep I'd started to think he was, I was ashamed to admit it. But yes, I was glad he was going to be there to hear me sing.

About ten minutes after I hung up from my father, the phone rang again.

"Lahni," my mother called from the kitchen. "It's for you, hon."

"Hello," I said, picking up. I was still in the study, thinking about my father. I thought it might be him calling back.

"Little sister, we got to find some time to rehearse. Get you back in shape."

"When, Marcus?" Thank God he was calling me. I knew he was disappointed in how I'd sung at the dress rehearsal. I was afraid he wouldn't want to have anything to do with the competition until Friday when he played, or worse, he'd make an excuse and back out completely.

"I'm thinking we can go over it once or twice tomorrow after church and the same thing on Thursday after choir rehearsal. We shouldn't have to do that much. You know the song. It's a matter of shakin' the heebie-jeebies out of you so you have more confidence in yourself."

"I know it will be better, Marcus."

"Oh, I know it will too, little sister, or you will have proven me wrong about you. And I'm not in the mood to be proven wrong this month. You know what I'm saying?"

The truth was, I was never totally sure what Marcus was saying, but this time I agreed immediately. If he felt I could do it, I would.

"I'll see you Sunday, Marcus. You'll hear the difference. You don't have to worry about being proven wrong."

"Who's worried?" the voice on the other end of the line asked. "Do I sound worried to you?"

CHAPTER TWENTY-SIX

"We need a dress! A gorgeous, stunning, red-carpet, Academy Award winning, incredible dress!" My mother was on a mission and I could barely keep up with her. It took us about three hours between Bloomingdale's, Saks, and a boutique called She's All That, which had dresses trimmed in anything shiny you could imagine. I said no to everything the girl working there showed us, but I thought I'd ask Carietta if she knew about it. She's All That was definitely more her style than mine.

In Bloomingdale's, though, we found a lavender dress that was very simple, but looked really good against my skin and fit the mood I was in, which was not flashy at all. This dress made me feel elegant like my mother looked when she got dressed up. It made me feel good about the way I looked in it, and that was all that mattered to me.

We also bought me a pair of heels that were a shade deeper than my dress. I argued, "We don't have to get these, Mom. When am I ever going to wear lavender shoes again?" But my mother insisted, "I don't really care if you wear them again or not, Lahni. This is a once in a lifetime occasion. So if you wear them only once in your life, it's perfectly all right with me."

I had never thought of my mother as extravagant until that Saturday afternoon. I realized as she whisked me around Bloomingdale's, she would have bought me just about anything in the store she thought would have encouraged me to go onstage Friday night at The Darby School. Just before we left, my mother wailed as though she'd seen a fire on the other side of the store. "Ohhhh!"

"What's the matter?" My heart jumped. I was ready to run with her to the nearest exit.

"We should get something to put in your hair!" She made a sharp right and raced across the floor to the hair-accessories boutique. I followed her, frowning. *She's gone crazy*, I thought. *Crazy*.

At first glance, I knew I wasn't interested in any of the satin bows or feathered combs. "Mom, I don't like any of these. Can we go now? Aren't you tired?"

"Wait, Lahni," she said firmly, and I knew there was no arguing. We were going to spend time in this department until she was satisfied I didn't need anything from it.

She marched over to a woman who was behind a display counter, leaning on it, looking bored. I stood several feet behind my mother, wondering how long it would take before she gave up.

"Excuse me, we're looking for a comb to put in my daughter's hair for a special occasion." I knew this was my cue. I didn't want to spoil the morning for her by being obstinate. She'd been so generous, the least I could do was play along until she felt the same way I did. I went and stood beside her at the counter.

"We just bought a lavender dress and shoes to match," Mom continued, shoulder to shoulder with me, "but I still think we need something for her hair."

"Everything we have is pretty much what you see here." The woman was too old to be working at this counter, I thought. All of the combs were so trendy looking. There wasn't anything there my mother would have bought for herself, and the saleswoman was much older than my mother. They needed someone about twenty, I thought, who was actually wearing one of the combs to help sell them.

"Do you have anything lavender? Maybe something with an amethyst stone?"

The saleswoman waved her hands over the display counter blankly. "Like I said, ma'am, everything we have is pretty much right here."

In the state my mother was in, it may have been hard for her to see what was so obvious to me. The woman wasn't any more interested in going out of her way to show anything from her counter than I was to wear them. But whatever picture of me my mother had in her head for Friday night was not going to be canceled out by some saleslady at Bloomingdale's who couldn't have cared less.

"So you don't have any suggestions at all for what would be good with a lavender silk dress?"

The woman glared at my mother. She had feathery white hair in a short, little boy's haircut and was wearing a navy and white striped shirt and a navy blue pair of pants. She should have been upstairs in the women's lingerie department, linens, or stationery. As if she were teaching a four year old the proper way to give information in a department store, she asked my mother in this silly voice, "What color hair does she have? What is her complexion like? Dark? Pale? Is it like yours?"

My mother looked at the woman coldly. She said, "This is my daughter, right here. This is who we're buying the clips for."

The woman's face colored a deep plum under her white bangs. "Oh." She forced an embarrassed chuckle. "I didn't hear you say this was your daughter. Did you say that?"

My mother looked at me. I could see a faint, satisfied smile on her face. "I don't know whether I said it or not. She was here, standing beside me, and I said 'we,' so I assumed you understood I was talking about her and me. *She's* the one who needs the clips."

"Yes. I understand," the woman said crisply. "So, do you see anything you like, dear?" she said to me.

I sighed. Shopping had stopped being fun. Now I just wanted to spend some more time with my mother, being excited about what we'd already bought and trying it on again when we got home. "No," I said flatly. "I don't see anything I like." I looked at my mother. "Are you ready?"

My mother looked at the saleswoman once again, as if there was more she might like to have said to her if I weren't there. But she put her arm around me, and "let's go, sweetheart" was all that came out.

CHAPTER TWENTY-SEVEN

Sunday, after church, we went over my song twice. The first time, I waited for Marcus to give me criticism, but after a couple of minutes he said, "All right, you ready?" I said yes and we went through it again. Each time, I heard a difference in what *he* was doing, and it was beautiful. There would be clusters of notes I hadn't heard before as though he were shading a drawing he was working on. But I wasn't going to try anything new at this point. I just concentrated on sounding stronger, more sure of myself.

After we finished the second time, Marcus told me, "You got to remember, Lahni. When they call your name, it will be *your* time to tell *your* story. It's not a race, you don't have to hurry through it. But you don't want to sing like you're crawling through mud, either. Ride the music. Listen to the signals I give you on the piano and don't just hear 'em with your ears. Hear 'em inside. What part of your story is this?" He played a few chords from the beginning. "And what part of your story is this?" He played a few chords from the chorus. "Can you feel 'em touch different parts of you?"

"Yes," I answered, but that was easy. Something always moved in me when Marcus played. It never really occurred to me to let it affect my singing that much. If I did, I wasn't sure I could concentrate on the words in the same way.

As though he were reading my mind, Marcus said, "You know the words. All you have to do is connect them with your own story and your own story with the music, and trust me, your voice will do the rest."

In all the days in class, Mr. Faringhelli had never told us anything like this. It didn't sound easy at all, but it made sense to me. I knew if I worked on it slowly, by myself, I could make the connections like he said.

When Mr. Faringhelli saw me in school on Monday, he asked me, "Lahni, who is your accompanist? He's pretty cool! Where'd you find him?" He sounded like a kid excited about a new CD.

"I sing in a church choir. He's our director."

"What church is it? If you've got playing like *that,* I'd consider going myself."

"Church of the Good Shepherd."

Mr. Faringhelli nodded. "I'll keep it in mind. I can't wait to hear him play again."

I realized Mr. Faringhelli hadn't said a word about my singing, and I certainly wasn't going to ask him. Obviously he hadn't been too impressed with it, only with the piano playing accompanying it.

I don't think I heard a word Marcus said all through choir practice Thursday night. He even said to me once, after he'd explained something about where the second sopranos were supposed to come in, "You got that, Miss Lahni?"

"Yes," I answered, knowing the only thing I'd been listening to was myself singing "His Eye Is on the Sparrow" in my head. It had been like that all day. I'd come from school, where I hadn't heard anything anyone had said to me, to choir practice, where the only thing I could think about was rehearsing my song. Katie had shrugged and said, "You're hopeless, Lahni," after asking me what I was wearing for the competition three times and having me answer, "Huh?" each time. "I guess I'll just have to show up tomorrow to see," she'd sighed.

Carietta stayed after choir practice to hear me rehearse, which made me extra nervous. After I'd sung once, Marcus folded his hands and put them on the piano. My heart sank.

Marcus doodled at the piano while he was speaking, all kinds of variations on the melody of "His Eye Is on the Sparrow." "Tomorrow night, Lahni, you can't be so stingy. You hear me?"

I stared at him, not having the slightest idea what he meant.

"You got to remember to share. This isn't all for you, or you could sing it to yourself in your bedroom. No, you're there on the stage to witness. Be a witness, a truthful witness, Lahni, and no matter what the judges say, you'll have won."

When Marcus was finished, Carietta seemed to know from my face that I wasn't sure how to take in what Marcus had just said. She put her arm around my shoulder. "You're going to be everything you need to be, Miss Lahni. Girl, you are going to knock the walls down and set the roof on fire!"

I smiled. Sure, I was. I could just imagine me singing and that happening. It would mean I'd have to have a voice like *hers* for somebody to say that. Carietta gave me a little gift-wrapped package. "This is for tomorrow night—"

"But you are coming, aren't you?" I asked her anxiously.

Carietta gave her neck a swivel. "I intend to be front row center. But I wanted you to have this in advance."

"Thank you, so much. Should I open it now?" The package was wrapped in pink, shiny paper with smiling moons and stars on it.

"Yes, you should. To see if you can use it tomorrow night."

I unwrapped the package. Inside the wrapping was a long, red velvet box. I opened the box.

"Oh!" I gasped. Nestled in folds of satin was a strand of pearls.

"People don't wear pearls like they used to. You might think they're kind of old-fashioned. But I think every girl ought to have some in her jewelry box, just in case the mood hits her. What color is your dress?"

"Lavender."

"Last time I looked, pearls and lavender were a good combination. Whatcha think, Mr. Delacroix?"

"Uh-huh." Marcus kept playing the chords of "His Eye Is on the Sparrow." I wondered if he was worried about me.

I hugged Carietta. "Thank you. I'll try to make you proud." But I meant it for both of them. I looked at the two of them and thought how I hadn't known them very long. Before them, I hadn't known even *one* black person very well. And I was black. African American. I remembered what my mother had told me. "There are lots of people who are confused, about who they are and what they are." I didn't think I was one of those people. And I thought it had something to do with getting to know Marcus and Carietta. I was glad they'd both be there for the competition. It was important to me that they be there, no matter what happened.

When I got home, my mom said there was a message from my father. I went to the answering machine and pressed the play button. After a long silence I heard his voice say, "Lahni . . . I'm calling after nine thirty because you said you'd be there. (Big sigh.) Apparently you're not. Well . . . I will . . . uh . . . be there . . . at your school . . . tomorrow . . . for the . . . uh . . . talent program . . . uh . . . competition . . . all right." CLICK.

I looked at the phone and I could see his face. I wanted to ask him, "Why Dad? Why does it have to be so hard?"

My mom called down from her room, "Is everything okay?"

"Yes, Mom," I answered, "he just called to say he was coming." Even though I knew she'd probably already heard the message.

CHAPTER TWENTY-EIGHT

From then on it seemed like everything went in slow motion except my mind. Friday, I barely spoke to anyone other than Katie all day. It was Katie who came to the bathroom with me between classes when I thought I was going to be sick. She also reassured me at least a dozen times that day that a curly Afro could definitely dry in the hours between when I set it after school and when I had to be back that night. And she guaranteed that no matter what color stage lights were on me, the lavender against my brown skin would be flattering. Best of all, she was on the alert for when Donna or any of the others were getting too close, and we'd hurry in the opposite direction when they did. Amber, of course, had taken the day off. What Broadway star would come to school when she had to perform that night?

On the way home, Katie asked me, "Do you want me to come home with you and help with anything?"

I laughed. "What are you, a glutton for punishment?" Katie laughed too. "No thanks," I told her. "I really appreciate what you did today, though. I'm sure it seemed like you were with some kind of shock-treatment patient."

"I can't wait to hear you, Lahni." Katie gave me a thumbs-up and pulled away on her bike. She stopped suddenly and turned around. "Hey, Lahni, what happened to that guy you were having the date with? Am I ever gonna know who he is?"

"Yep," I laughed. I'd forgotten completely that I'd ever teased her about my mystery date. "He's playing for me in the competition."

"Are you serious?" Katie's eyes were as big as dessert plates.

"Let's put it this way. I asked a good friend of mine if he'd accompany me—on the piano—and he said yes. As far as I'm concerned, that's the only kind of date I'm interested in right now. Got it?"

"Oh. You weren't serious. You were only kidding." Katie looked very disappointed that she wasn't going to hear about a secret boyfriend.

"No, I'm very serious. And so is he. Wait till you hear him." I waved to her and kept pedaling. I'd meant it.

Marcus Delacroix was the best date I could think of. Every time I thought about him, I smiled.

My mother helped me put in dozens of tiny rollers for the huge, curly Afro I wanted. An hour later, I'd gone through "His Eye Is on the Sparrow" a hundred times, like a CD on instant replay.

I went to my mother's bedroom and knocked on the door. "Mom?"

"Come on in." She was lying across the bed. Bad sign number one was that there were crumpled tissues next to her. Bad sign number two was that her eyes were red and puffy.

"Mom, are you all right?"

"Of course, honey. Are you?"

"Sure."

"What did you want to ask me?"

"I don't think it's such a great time."

"Why? Because it's something about your father and me?"

"Yes."

"Well, it can't be anything I haven't thought of." She sniffed and laughed. "What's on your mind? I don't want anything on your mind except doing well tonight, so tell me. What is it?"

"I didn't know . . . if you were going to . . . I mean,

you're probably not going to sit with each other, are you?"

My mother chuckled. "I swear, you're a mind reader, Lahni Schuler." She sat up and leaned against the headboard. "Tell me, would you be very upset if we didn't sit together?"

"I don't know. I figured there was a pretty good chance you wouldn't be."

My mother scooted to the side of the bed where I was and swung her legs around so that we were sitting side by side. "I don't really know what to do, Lahni. I don't want you to be embarrassed. I know your classmates will be there, and your teachers. Tell me the truth. It really would make it easier for you if we sat next to each other tonight and pretended, wouldn't it?"

I thought about how the last time they saw each other, they hadn't even said three words. How could they sit together in the Darby auditorium and pretend they were still happily married?

"No, Mom. It's silly. You should do what you want to do. There is one thing, though . . ."

"Sure, Lahni. What is it?"

"Could you please . . . not get into a fight?"

My mother put her arms around me and kissed my cheek. "I won't embarrass you. *We* won't embarrass you. You have my word."

I went down to the study to watch television, hoping it would keep my mind off the competition and how my parents would behave toward one another. There was this old movie on called *Cleopatra,* starring Elizabeth Taylor. She was very beautiful except I couldn't understand how anybody thought she looked Egyptian. When it was over, I went up to the bathroom and tried doing my version of her eye makeup with my mother's eyeliner and shadows. At least it gave me a good laugh to see me standing in my father's old undershirt, with my hair in a hundred little rollers and my eyes painted like a mannequin in the window of Miss Edna's Beauty Salon. If anyone could've gotten away with those Magic Marker eyebrows and gold eyelids, it was Carietta Chisolm. She was actually almost there already. But it certainly wasn't me. The most I could hope for, for my big night, was a little lavender shadow, mascara, and lip gloss.

My mom knocked on the bathroom door. "Hon, I have to run to the store for a minute. Do you need anything?'

I opened the door and watched her expression. "Oh no, Lahni! You can't wear that much makeup on your eyes! I don't mean to hurt your feelings, sweetheart, but I think you have on waaay too much shadow and eyeliner—and all that gold! Honey, maybe it's your nerves. Do you want me to help you when I come back?"

I put my hands over my mouth, but I couldn't control

myself. I hooted with laughter. I sat on the side of the tub, doubled over.

"Lahni, you think you're sooo funny, don't you? And I thought you were serious! I thought, my Lord, she thinks she looks nice and what am I going to do?"

"Well, you did it Mom; your face said everything. You mean you don't like my Cleopatra makeup? I wanted to look like Elizabeth Taylor!"

"You're bonkers, Lahni, that's what you are. I think it *is* your nerves. You've gone right around the bend."

I stood up, still panting and holding my stomach.

"I've got to go out for a minute. Is it safe to leave you alone?" My mother held out a washcloth for me.

"I don't know. I think it looks really nice myself. Egyptian."

"Yeah, it's Egyptian all right." She leaned over to kiss me. She smelled like her favorite perfume, Dior. Then she squeezed my head so tight, I thought my rollers would explode.

I washed my face, still laughing to myself. While I was making sure all of the traces of Cleopatra were gone, I had a brainstorm. I threw the towel on the sink, ran down to the study, and picked up the phone.

"Information for New York City, please. Could I have the number of the Mayfair Hotel? Thank you."

When the voice answered, I pictured the man I'd seen my father speaking to at the main desk. I thought of the lobby and the big arm chairs and us sitting next to each other for over an hour not speaking.

"Hello? Could you connect me with Mr. Timothy Schuler's room, please. I remembered the red and gold wallpaper in the living room of what my father called his apartment.

"There doesn't seem to be any answer. Would you like to leave a message?"

"No, thank you." I hung up. Why couldn't he have been there? Then I looked at the clock. Of course. I dialed again, a number I knew by heart.

"Ruth?" It was my father's secretary. She'd known me since I was a baby. "Hi, Ruth, this is Lahni Schuler. Is my dad there? Thanks. No, I can wait." I held the phone, thinking about calls my mother had made to him in the past, asking him if he was going to be able to get home for something they'd planned. Most of the time, if she had to make the call, it already meant that he wasn't coming. I'd hear her ask him, "Well, when were you going to tell me? Was I just supposed to be here thinking we were going, when you knew all along we weren't?" I wondered if Stupid Pat was in his life then? I wondered what he'd told Stupid Pat about tonight?

"Lahni?" He sounded like I was the last person in the world he expected to hear from.

"Hi, Dad."

"Is something wrong?"

What a way to start, I thought. *No, nothing's wrong, but it's not as though everything is super great, either.* "No. I called to speak to you about tonight."

"I called last night like I said I would. I left a message. Did you get it?"

"Of course I got it, Dad."

"Lahni, where were you that late on a school night? What's going on there?"

"*Nothing's* going on. I was at rehearsal. Like I said."

"Well, I hope this thing isn't messing up your schoolwork."

"My schoolwork is fine. Dad, I called to ask you something."

"Yes?"

"I want to ask you something about Mom."

There was silence. I was trying to figure out what to say to fill it when he asked, "What about your mother, Lahni?"

Nothing to do but spit it out, I thought. "I keep thinking how strange it will be that both of you will be there, but you'll be sitting separately. I haven't told anybody that you've . . . moved, so I guess all my teachers and the dean and everybody will figure it out when they see . . ."

Another silence. This one was longer than the last. Finally he said very quietly, "Did you talk about this with your mother?'

"A little. I just told her I didn't want you to fight."

"We won't fight. We wouldn't do that." He said it as though they'd never fought.

"I know. I was wondering about the sitting together thing, I guess, and I thought it couldn't hurt to ask."

"No, of course, you can ask. I'm actually sorry you thought you *had* to ask."

"Well, I'm sorry to interrupt you at work." I knew I should let him go, even though I didn't want to.

"Lahni, we'll fix it, okay? Your mother and I will fix it." I wanted to ask him if he meant their marriage, the whole thing, but I knew he probably was only talking about them getting along together that night.

"Thanks, Dad."

"I'll see you later, right?"

"Yes. Thank you."

"Don't keep thanking me, Lahni. I'll be there because you're my daughter and I love you. All right?"

"Yes." And why did I still want to thank him again? Maybe because even if the competition were suddenly canceled, it would have been worth it to hear him say what he just did.

CHAPTER TWENTY-NINE

Before now, I'd done a good job of keeping myself from thinking about who might actually win. I hadn't heard either Amber or Lisa sing solo. Amber was beyond confident. She had probably already cleared a place in her room for the trophy. But quiet, beautiful Lisa just might fool everyone. Her father was accompanying her on violin, and Mr. Faringhelli said she came from a musical family. I bet she was going to sing from an opera or something and have the judges weeping and saying she was a prodigy and they should give her a full scholarship to a college to study voice.

But, hey, at least I was going to show up. At that moment, between feeling vaguely nauseous and a little dizzy, I couldn't imagine anything but trying to get through the song, listening to the words, and trying to connect to them like Marcus had said. If I could pull that off and stay on pitch, too, I'd be grateful. I didn't want to let anyone down, but I couldn't guarantee any prizes, either.

When the doorbell rang, I started to ignore it. I'd just spoken to my father, my mother was on some kind of errand, and it was too early to expect Marcus. I sneaked behind the drapes in the living room to see who it was.

"Lahni!" I could hear Katie calling. "Lahni, it's me, Katie!"

I looked through the screen door at her. She looked as if she wasn't sure I was going to let her in.

"Hey," she said timidly. "Timid" wasn't a word you'd usually associate with Katie.

I opened the screen door.

"I know you said you didn't need any help, but I thought I'd come over in case something unexpected came up."

I laughed. "Yeah, like my rollers are too tight. Do you want to help me loosen every single one of 'em before my head explodes?"

Katie bounced in. Immediately she was her old, loud self. "You're right! I've never seen you in rollers. You must have a couple hundred up there."

"That's what it feels like. I told my mom I want the world's biggest Afro tonight."

Katie put her hands over her mouth, screaming into them. "Ohmygodohmygodohmygod!"

"I thought it's the one thing neither one of the other girls will be able to do—show up with a huge Afro."

Katie squealed and fell backward onto the living room floor, rolling from side to side. I sat on a chair in front of her and thoroughly enjoyed being so entertaining, even if it was in my living room and not in the auditorium. Katie sat up and folded her legs in front of her. "I'm sorry. I didn't mean to act like such an idiot. I'm just so excited about tonight."

I don't know why I said what I did next. I think it was because I felt really close to her at that moment and I wanted to say what else was on my mind besides singing that night.

"Katie, I thought you should know, in case you notice anything strange tonight about how my parents act, that they're separated." I held myself very still. I didn't know if the nausea now was from nervousness about singing or what I'd just said.

Katie's face got very pink and her eyes widened. "They are?"

I nodded.

"But they're both coming tonight?"

I nodded again.

"When you say separated, you mean your father doesn't live here anymore or are you and your mother going to move out?"

"He's already gone. He lives in New York."

"Whoa! I'm really sorry, Lahni."

"I am glad they're both going to be there tonight. I just hope I don't make an idiot out of myself, and I hope they can get along long enough to get through it."

"Is it that bad?"

Suddenly I realized I'd said all that I wanted Katie to know. She had to have realized it wasn't that easy to tell her what I had.

"We probably shouldn't talk about it anymore. My mom went out for something, but she'll be right back. I don't want to be in the middle of talking about them when she walks in. She'd know right away, and I'd feel like a jerk telling you something that's probably not my business to tell you."

"I'm glad you did, Lahni. I always tell you how bad my parents' fights are, and you always listen to me go on and on." Katie put her head down and I heard sniffling.

"Oh, no," I said standing in front of her. "No falling apart tonight. We can't. You'll get hives or whatever that is you get when you cry, and then you won't be able to come see how my Afro looks on stage."

Katie stood up, wiped her nose with her hand, and giggled. "I'm such a fool," she said.

"A fool with a snotty nose. Ewww! Get a tissue, fast!" I told her. And we laughed. But I still felt like I was twenty years older than her. I knew how afraid she was whenever her parents fought, and now she'd probably be more afraid. I thought how I wouldn't wish a parents' marriage coming apart on any kid, especially a girl like Katie, who'd probably be hurt for the rest of her life.

Katie wanted to stay and help me get dressed, but I wouldn't let her. I wanted privacy. Once she was gone, though, I went upstairs to pull out my dress and shoes. I was too sweaty to put them on, and it was also a little early, but I wanted to hold the dress up to me and try on the shoes. This, I decided, would help me get my focus back on tonight.

The dress was fine, gorgeous. I liked it better each time I looked at it. But when I tried on the shoes, they felt a little snug. They hadn't felt snug at all at the store, and my mother had asked me a dozen times how they felt.

I knew I had no choice now but to wear them, snug or not. Maybe if I put lotion on my feet, I thought. I took off my jeans, my dad's old T-shirt, and my bra and started putting aloe moisturizer on my legs and feet.

I saw myself in the mirror. My bare legs, my stomach,

my breasts. My mother said I was beautiful. A beautiful, African American . . . what? Girl? Teenager? Young woman? Of course, she was my mother. Was it ridiculous to hope that one day somebody else would think so too? Somebody who wasn't crazy or confused?

I put my jeans, my dad's T-shirt, and my new shoes back on. I went downstairs and sat in the living room. The shoes still felt awfully snug.

I got on the floor and lay on my back, trying to sing the words of my song without using my voice too much. Impossible. Couldn't be done. I decided to hum instead, all the while thinking I might have to run to the bathroom and be sick.

My mother barely got inside before she called to me, "Great! Great! Great! You're exactly where you're supposed to be. Now all you have to do is get up and sit right there on the couch!"

She didn't look especially upset about anything, but she was definitely excited. I did as I was told. Right away she dropped her bag next to us and began pulling out my rollers. "Mom! What are you doing?"

"I'm only taking out the first few rows. I've got something to show you. And besides, it's almost time for you to get dressed anyway. Don't squirm, and close your eyes. You can't look."

I heard her rustling around in her shopping bag, and I knew she'd gone back for those velvet bows she'd seen at Bloomingdale's. I didn't want to wear bows in my hair—there was no way I was going to wear bows in my hair—but I didn't know how to put my foot down without hurting her feelings. To make it worse, as soon as she finished putting them in, she gushed, "Ooooh! Oh my!"

I wanted to sink right through the couch.

"Okay. Now we're going upstairs to the mirror," she said. "You can open your eyes, but you can't put your hand up there to see what I did."

I slipped out of my new shoes and followed her upstairs. She went straight into my room and rushed to open the closet door where there was a full-length mirror. "Now, close your eyes again before you come in."

She led me to the mirror. "Okay, you can open your eyes."

To say I was surprised would be an understatement. Mostly, I guess, because I was expecting those velvet bows. But it was also because I never wear anything in or on my hair other than headbands to make it lie down or keep it off my forehead if I'm breaking out. I didn't think I'd like anything my mother had bought to put in my hair.

But when I saw the two combs with four, small

amethyst stones on each, I couldn't quite believe it. I didn't look like a six-year-old girl going to a birthday party, and I didn't look like I'd spent hours sticking things into my hair as if it were a nest to be decorated. No, there on either side of my curly Afro were two beautiful combs that framed my face and made me—yes!—elegant looking.

"Oh!" Now *I* said it, and I remembered how similar my mother had sounded a moment ago. "They're really beautiful."

"Yes, they are," my mother agreed. "But then, what'd you expect? They're on my daughter. Now you have some new jewelry to wear with your new dress."

I suddenly remembered the pearls Carietta had given me. I hadn't told my mother about them.

"I forgot to tell you. Carietta gave me a pearl necklace to wear too. It was a good-luck present."

My mother looked very surprised at first. Then she said, "Well, if you think it's too much, the combs and the necklace, my feelings won't be hurt." But I knew they would.

"They won't be too much. I'm sure of it." I looked again at the combs. "They're wonderful. I love them." My mom patted my shoulder and left. She knew I didn't wear jewelry that much, so the combs and the necklace would be more than she'd probably ever see me in.

The one piece of jewelry I thought I'd always keep, and didn't ever wear because I thought it might get damaged or lost, was the bracelet from my father. It was the one he'd given me for graduation from lower school, the thin braid of gold with the six tiny pearls on it. I opened my jewelry box and there it was. I picked it up and remembered my father putting it on me for the first time.

I laughed. Hair combs. Pearl necklace. Gold bracelet. For someone who never wore jewelry, I'd feel like a Christmas tree. No. I'd think of them all as good-luck charms. I'd be one, big ol' good-luck charm in a dress, with the world's biggest Afro and lavender shoes that were too tight.

CHAPTER THIRTY 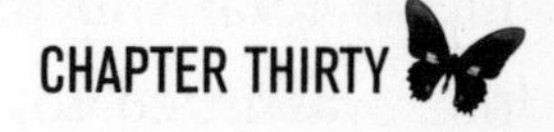

"Lahni! Marcus is here!"

You'd have thought he was my prom date. Mom and Marcus were at the bottom of the stairs, waiting for me to come to the top.

I wouldn't have wanted to look any other way. My dress was trés cool. My hair was gigantic, perfectly round, and the combs looked like they were designed especially for my Afro. My shoes were still a little pinchy—I was positive we'd bought the wrong size—but I didn't care in the least. Who would know as long as I didn't limp? Tomorrow morning, we could return them if we wanted. I would have worn them four or five hours, tops. Girls at school bragged they'd returned shoes after wearing them four or five months. Besides, the heels were too high for me anyway. I felt like I was walking on stilts.

I walked to the top of the stairs and struck a Naomi Campbell. I didn't look down at Mom and Marcus because when I did, I was planning to look surprised, like, *Oh, my goodness, I didn't know* you'd *be there!* and all the time they'd be staring up at how fabulous I looked.

But when I did look down, I didn't have to fake surprise at all. One glance at Marcus Delacroix III put me in total shock. He was wearing a silver-gray suit that was fitted to his chubby body so that it looked like all the fat was muscle. But the shirt and tie topped the suit. His shirt was pink satin and his tie a deeper pink with glittery purple stripes. And, of course, his dark glasses.

It wasn't my father's taste for sure, and it might not have been mine or anyone else's but Marcus's. Suddenly it made sense why he'd asked me what color my dress was. I didn't know whether he'd bought the shirt and tie for tonight or whether he'd pulled it out of the hundreds he owned. It didn't matter. What was unmistakable was that he'd dressed for me, so that we would complement each other, and I couldn't have been more proud.

"Marcus!" It was all I could say for the moment.

"Wait, little sister, don't open your mouth. You've got

plenty of time for that. Let me do the talking." He leaned back like he did at choir rehearsal and put his ringed fingers under his chin like he was praying. "You are a sensation, Miss Lahni Schuler. I have seen many a beautiful young woman in my time, but you are truly, truly special. From the fierce jeweled Afro to the killer heels, you are a sight to behold. God bless you and keep you tonight. Amen and amen!"

Mom jumped up and down with her hands over her mouth like a little girl. I smiled, but I still couldn't get over how Marcus looked. I'd never thought of him as handsome before, just talented and my friend. But tonight he was handsome in his own spectacular way, and I wanted him to know I thought so.

I went to the bottom of the stairs. "Marcus, you're the one who looks *gorgeous*! I am so excited we're gonna be on that stage together tonight, I don't care what happens."

"Well, I do," Marcus snapped. "As my mama used to say, 'Pretty is as pretty does.' And I want us to make some very pretty music tonight."

"Amen and amen!" my mother said.

Mom and Marcus had decided he'd drive me to school because we were supposed to be there early. I wished in a way she was coming with us because

I wasn't sure what was happening with my father. Would they meet there? Would he be there when she got there? What if she got there first and was already sitting alone and there was no seat for him? Would he sit separately from her anyway and pretend he had no choice? I wanted more than anything for this not to be a night that caused her pain.

CHAPTER THIRTY-ONE

We pulled into the Darby parking lot. "Marcus," I gasped, "please stop. I'm gonna be sick."

Marcus stopped. I jumped out of the car and was sick right there in the parking lot. Luckily, I was careful not to mess up my dress or shoes. I leaned way over, even though it was hard to keep my balance. Marcus got out and came around to where I was. "Little sister?"

"Yuk," I said, breathing heavily. I was pretty certain I was finished, but I couldn't have been more humiliated. "Marcus, don't look. I'm sooo sorry."

"Could you tell me what you have to be sorry about?" There was a shout in Marcus's voice even though he was whispering. "You got a mighty bad case of the jitters, though."

I felt weak and still a little dizzy, but I could stand up straight now. "I didn't expect that to happen."

"No, I didn't think it was planned. 'Cause if it was, you were taking a mighty big chance on ruinin' that Paris gown you got on."

I couldn't laugh, but I managed to smile.

"Now, if you're finished, would you mind gettin' back into the car so we can find a parking spot far away from where we're standing. Let's pretend that was one of the *other* girls with a case of bad nerves."

I did a quick check to see if my dress and shoes really were all right and then got back into the car.

"In all seriousness," Marcus said, "if you don't think this is the right night for you to be tryin' to win a medal with your singing, we can go right back the same way we came."

"Marcus, I'm not a quitter. I came here to be in this competition, and I'm gonna be."

Marcus looked at me as he pulled into a parking space. "I knew that, little sister. I most definitely knew that."

When we were walking toward the entrance to the auditorium, Marcus stopped and pulled something out of his pocket. "Here," he said, and held out his hand. "You could probably use this." It was a stick of gum. "I'd give you some mouthwash if I had it, but I don't usually carry it around with me."

"Thanks, Marcus. I hope I remember to take it out before I sing."

"If not, it won't be the first time I've seen a singer in a silk dress and fancy shoes stick a wad of gum behind her ear before she cut loose. Little sister, I've seen the best of 'em do it." Marcus let out his hoarse laugh and waved his ringed fingers. "Shoot. All we need you to do tonight is sing! Don't worry 'bout the gum placement!"

We walked into the empty auditorium, and I looked at it as if for the first time. It seemed huge, like the Roman Colosseum, except with a roof on it. I didn't even want to think what it would be like with people in all those seats, and I hoped I wouldn't be anywhere around when they started to fill the room. I knew it would be full, because before the competition, the Darby orchestra would be playing and there were sixty girls in it. All of their parents and their friends will be here, I thought, and somewhere among them, my parents, too. I put my hand on my stomach as if I could really control the feeling that there were little people bouncing on trampolines at the bottom of it.

Mike, the custodian, was mopping the floor. Mike was one of the custodians who was known for being unfriendly. He didn't speak to any students that I knew of. Tonight he stopped his mopping to say, "Hello, hello," with an accent I didn't even know he had. Maybe he was Polish or Russian.

I nodded. Mike said, "How are you?" as though we were newly acquainted neighbors. "Tonight we have good music, huh? I like good music."

I smiled blankly. Now I had to worry about whether Mike, the custodian who'd never said two words to me before, thought I did well.

Mr. Faringhelli came out onto the stage. Lisa and her father followed him.

"Lahni! You look wonderful!" Mr. Faringhelli didn't look so bad himself. A black suit, white shirt, and tie definitely wasn't his usual rumpled, but cute look. Instead, he was dashing.

I couldn't help myself. "You do too, Mr. Faringhelli!"

"Actually," he said, coming to the front of the empty stage with Lisa and her father still trailing behind him, "I look like a funeral director. But it's the only suit I have, and I wanted to look like a grown-up for you young ladies." He turned and smiled at Lisa, then turned right back to me.

Lisa stood next to Mr. Faringhelli, looking down at me from the stage. "Lahni, your hair is awesome. You should always wear it like that."

"Thanks," I said, feeling self-conscious. "You look fantastic."

Her father, in a light brown suit, was carrying his violin in a worn, peeling, black leather case. He looked like a doctor or a businessman, I thought, who'd found a violin and was looking for its owner. I couldn't imagine him playing the violin in a performance, much less accompanying Lisa. But who was I to talk? Already they'd all looked behind me to Marcus, in his satin shirt and glitter tie. And, of course, his dark glasses.

"This is Marcus. He's playing the piano." Now I really felt like the world's biggest idiot. I didn't know what else to say. "Accompanist" didn't seem like enough, but I knew "playing the piano" was totally wrong too.

Mr. Faringhelli practically fell off the stage trying to reach out to shake Marcus's hand. "I didn't get a chance to tell you last week how great you are."

"That's very kind," Marcus said, looking and sounding like he was one of those men who sang in the old groups my mother loved, the Four Tops or the Temptations. I'd forgotten how smooth Marcus could sound when you first met him.

"Lahni told me you're the music director at a church in the area. I told her your playing was enough to make me want to join whatever church that is." I'd never seen Mr. Faringhelli act like this before. He looked like a kid, grinning and nodding his head again and again. Lisa, smiling slightly, was watching him too.

Her father stepped forward and extended his hand to

Marcus. "Henry Shin," he said a little stiffly. They shook hands, and then Mr. Shin shook mine and stepped back next to Lisa.

She had to be one of the most beautiful girls at Darby. I'd thought it before, but tonight I was convinced. She was wearing a white linen dress that was perfectly plain. It was so simple and yet so exquisite, she could have gotten married in it. Her long black hair wasn't curled tonight; it hung straight down her back. When I looked at her closely, I could see that she had very pale eye shadow on and about four tubes of mascara. Her eyes were enormous to begin with, and tonight they looked like headlights with lashes.

Now that I was there, Mr. Faringhelli went over for both Lisa and me where we should go once we were onstage. I could tell he was a little annoyed that Amber wasn't there yet. "It would help if Amber were here," he said, looking at his watch. "But I'll let her know all this whenever she decides to show up." He told us the order we'd be singing in. "Now, you know, of course, that the Darby orchestra will go on first. We had to figure out a way to fill out the program, and that's what the dean came up with, so that's what's happening. Then there'll be a slight break where I come out and talk about the talent competition and each of you. Oh, and the judges, of course."

The judges. I'd totally forgotten about the judges. In

the beginning I'd worried about who they were, and then I forgot all about them.

"Then, Lisa, you'll open," Mr. Faringhelli continued. "Then Amber. Then Lahni. After the three of you have finished, there'll be another short break while the judges make their decision. You three will go across the hall to a classroom to wait; hopefully, that will make you less nervous than waiting backstage."

I'd been concentrating so much on being able to sing at all, the reality of competing in front of judges and waiting to hear the answer in the same night hadn't really hit me. But it was happening. In about forty-five minutes all of it was going to happen just as Mr. Faringhelli had said.

"Well, I can't say I hadn't started to worry, because I had." It was Mr. Faringhelli's way of greeting Amber, who came sweeping in as though she were at the Oscars. And I'm not kidding in the least. If anyone had suggested to me that I wear a gown to the Darby middle school talent competition, I would have laughed in their face. "Why would I want to make myself look like such a jerk?" I would have asked. And what if I lost? I'd have made my parents go out and buy a gown for me to lose a middle school competition in? Not in a million years.

But that's exactly what Amber had done. Not only

was she wearing a gown that I bet she'd made her parents buy just for tonight, but it was red and white striped. She looked like a candy cane. With too much makeup on. Not that Amber had any doubts about winning. I'm sure she fully expected to receive her trophy in her gown and make a speech like she really had won an Academy Award. I guess I had to give her credit. Everyone says that it's important in life to believe in yourself. At fourteen, she had that category sewn up. Nobody believed in Amber Merrill more than she did. And I hadn't even met her parents.

Amber didn't apologize for being late. But she did greet me with, "Hi Lahni. Your hair is soooo big! Is it a wig? If that's really your hair, you must have a ton of spray on it to stretch it out like that!"

There was a silence I could have filled by answering her, but I didn't. After the silence, Mr. Faringhelli went over all the details of the night again for Amber. She kept tossing her head and walking as though she were in a modeling competition instead of a talent one. I couldn't wait to hear what she was singing. *She probably has backup dancers hidden somewhere in the building,* I thought. *They're going to come onstage in the middle of her song and lift her up for a big finish.*

Amber had come so late that right behind her were the students who'd volunteered to usher that night. "You know what that means, folks," Mr. Faringhelli warned us as the girls came in, chattering. "We've got about fifteen minutes before we open the doors." I swallowed hard as yet another wave of nausea went through me. "Let me take you all across the hall to the classroom where you'll wait until the orchestra finishes playing. I thought about letting you sit in the audience with your folks if you wanted to, but I think that would be more nerve-racking than anything." If only he knew, I thought. I tried to guess where each of my parents was at that second, but I knew if I thought about it too long or too hard, I might get depressed. Or I might decide to go out and see for myself what was going on between them. Either way, I was better off trying not to think about them at all. If that was possible.

"Oh, I wouldn't mind sitting with my parents," Amber said breezily. "I just don't have anything to change into if I'm going to sit out there. And there's no decent place to change back into my gown when it's time for me to go on."

Lisa and I looked at each other and tucked our lips to keep from laughing out loud. Even Marcus and Lisa's father seemed to have traces of smiles. I could imagine Amber in a private dressing room down the hall changing from her "in the audience" outfit to her candy-cane gown while everyone waited for her to start the competition. Mr. Faringhelli made this face as though he had a sudden twinge of pain. "At any rate, I decided it was best for you to sit in the classroom across the hall; so that's where you'll be. I've got some sodas and water and cookies for you to munch on if anyone has an appetite." He smiled at Lisa and me and avoided looking at Amber. I wondered what their rehearsals had been like.

"Were you able to have the piano tuned since the dress rehearsal?" Marcus asked.

"Of course," answered Mr. Faringhelli. "I meant to mention that." Besides me not sounding that great at the rehearsal, the piano had not quite been up to Mr. Marcus's standards.

"Do you mind if I see what it sounds like, while we still have time?" Marcus asked.

"Absolutely!" Mr. Faringhelli told him. He hurried over to it and raised the lid. "We had it tuned this afternoon, so it should be in good shape."

We all watched as Marcus went to the side of the stage where the piano was already in place for the orchestra. He didn't sit at the bench like I expected him to. He just did what he did when he taught us parts at choir. His fingers brushed up and down the keyboard, playing clusters of notes, all of them making you want to hear more, but before you knew it, he was finished. "Thank you," he said huskily to Mr. Faringhelli.

"Oh, my pleasure, Mr. Delacroix." Mr. Faringhelli grinned. "My pleasure."

"Call me Marcus," Marcus rasped, and Mr. Faringhelli nodded and grinned like a six-year-old boy at a Macy's Thanksgiving Day Parade.

Two of the senior girls came up to the stage. "Mr. F," one of them said in a helpless, little girl voice, "what do you want us to do?"

Mr. Faringhelli answered, "Just a minute, Roz." He told us, "We better get you over to the classroom. We're getting close."

We followed him backstage to a side door that led to the hallway. Across the hall was one of the classrooms I remembered from when I first came to Darby. It was for the younger girls. Most of the middle and upper school girls had classes on the higher floors, with the exception of gym class.

Mr. Faringhelli seemed proud of the plates of cookies he'd set out, with different colored napkins and bottles of juice, soda, and water. It looked like he was giving us a party. I wondered if either Lisa or even Amber would have an appetite. Just then Amber gurgled, "Ooooooh, yummy!" and beamed a smile at Mr. Faringhelli. He smiled faintly and said to us, "I'll be back to check on you." Then he turned to leave when Mr. Shin said, "Uh, Mr. Faringhelli?"

"Yes sir?"

Mr. Shin set his violin case very carefully down on one of the desks. "You mentioned the judges. Who are they exactly? May we know?"

"Yeah," Amber chimed in. "My mother said I should find out who they are too."

Mr. Faringhelli looked past Amber to include all of us. "Of course you can know." He pulled a piece of paper out of his suit pocket. "This is my cheat sheet," he said, chuckling. "I don't know any of these people myself. The dean picked them." He opened the folded sheet of paper. "Let's see. There's Harry Klapson, the head of the music department at Connecticut State University, Myrna Schwartzchild, the director of the New Clarion Choral Society, and"—he put on a funny British accent—"our verrry special guest judge, Mrs. Daisy Clarke, the mayor's wife."

"I see," said Mr. Shin.

"Well, I don't know any of 'em," Marcus murmured.

Mr. Faringhelli refolded his piece of paper and put it back in his pocket. "Okay, I'm off. Like I said, I'll be back to keep you posted on how we're moving along. I'm sure you'll be able to hear the orchestra from here, though. You'll know when the first act is over." He propped the classroom door open with a wastepaper basket and went across the hall, into the auditorium. When he opened the door, I could hear the Darby orchestra warming up.

Mr. Faringhelli was right. I could hear a couple of songs from *A Chorus Line* that I recognized, and the applause of the audience was loud and enthusiastic. If what I heard was any indication, there were a lot of people across the hall.

Marcus had taken a seat at a desk and I sat next to him. If seeing Marcus Delacroix sitting at a kid's desk in a Darby School classroom wasn't strange enough, sitting next to him was absolutely science fiction. I asked him quietly, "Do you think any members of the choir will come?"

Marcus looked over his dark glasses at me. "Little sister, to hear you *and* me? For the first time onstage together? What do you think?"

I laughed. "I hope I don't disappoint them."

Marcus said, "I ain't worried. That thought never even crossed my mind."

"Okay, folks, we're at intermission. That'll be about ten minutes. I'll come back and get you in five so that you can get positioned backstage." Behind Mr. Faringhelli, I could see the members of the orchestra filing down the hallway, chattering excitedly about their performance. Girls were high-fiving each other and laughing, relieved that it had gone well and that it was over.

Mr. Faringhelli disappeared again inside the auditorium. Amber, who hadn't sat down for a moment and announced that it was because her gown would wrinkle, began to do a vocal warm up. She sang "oo oo oo oo oo" and "ah ah ah ah ah" and "ee ee ee ee ee" with a look on her face as though she had just been fitted for dentures and they didn't fit. Lisa and her father looked at each other and silently agreed to step out into the hall. Soon I heard Mr. Shin playing his violin. I didn't know for sure if it was the piece they were using for the competition, but whatever it was, it was truly beautiful. When Amber heard Mr. Shin, she stopped her warm-up immediately, and we could both hear Lisa singing softly along with the violin. I was pretty sure they were actually rehearsing the competition piece, because it was so magical the way Lisa's voice seemed to call to the violin, and the violin answered either higher or lower than Lisa had sung to it. Amber made a face like she was listening to a car wreck.

Marcus leaned over to me and said, "How 'bout you? You gonna find someplace to warm up your voice?" It was as though he'd said something I'd never heard of before or considered. Certainly when I sang with the choir, we did warm-ups. Even in Mr. Faringhelli's class we did warm-ups. But somehow I hadn't thought of warming up for the competition. "Yes," I said to him. "I'll go down the hall. I'll be right back."

"Take your time. Get yourself together. We're comin' up on an important moment. Center yourself."

I'd slipped out of my shoes and now had trouble putting them back on. Not only were they still tight, it felt like my feet had swollen, making them feel even tighter. I pushed into them and stood. They were the wrong shoes. I knew for sure now. Too high, too tight, and it was too late to do anything about it.

I left Marcus in the room and went to the end of the hallway, opposite from where Lisa and Mr. Shin had gone.

For a second I couldn't remember one single word of the song. Then when I did, I couldn't find my key. *Breathe. Like Mr. Faringhelli says. Breathe.* I did. I remembered that Marcus had said, "If it makes you feel comfortable to hum during the introduction to hear where your voice is, then hum. It's that kinda song and you can be that kinda singer." I hummed for a minute until I felt my voice was steady. Then I began to sing softly. I could still hear Lisa and her father at the other end of the hall, and Amber must have gotten louder, because even though I couldn't see her, it sounded like she was about three feet away. *Get yourself together. Center yourself.*

"Lahni?" It was Mr. Faringhelli. Marcus was there in the hallway and so were Amber, Lisa, and her father, with his violin. Mr. Faringhelli took a step toward me and smiled. "We're ready to go."

CHAPTER THIRTY-TWO

Fuchsia. The whole stage was lit in a bright fuchsia, which I took as a good-luck sign for both me and Marcus. There were fuchsia-colored stained glass windows at church, and I remembered watching Marcus play the piano and the organ in their light. He looked like a big, happy king. The same way he looked tonight.

Of course, Lisa would look wonderful under the lights too. I just wasn't sure how they'd make Amber's candy-cane gown look. And she was wondering too.

Standing right behind me, she moaned, "Ugh. Those lights are horrible. Mr. Faringhelli doesn't know what he's doing. They should have hired a professional who designs lights for Broadway shows."

I knew not to respond. I was determined not to answer anything she said because all of it was negative unless she was talking about Amber. Lisa and her father seemed to have come to the same conclusion. They stood a few feet away holding hands as we listened to Mr. Faringhelli make his introduction speech.

I'd only been onstage three times—all of them at Darby. I had played Lolabelle, a cow who refused to give milk until all the farm animals were treated fairly. That was in a play in third grade. And I'd sung twice in the Darby chorus for the holiday concert. But I'd never listened to an audience from backstage like I was listening now—it sounded as though it were one person with a thousand sets of hands. And some people you could pick out because they were louder than the rest. But most of them applauded as if they all had the same mind, starting and stopping together. Of course, I couldn't help but wonder where my parents were out there. Were they next to each other, side by side, and would that really be all right for both of them? Or was it some big sacrifice they were making for me and hating every minute of it?

"Our first performer tonight is Lisa Shin. Lisa will be singing a traditional Korean folk song. You can see the name of it in your program. I keep mispronouncing it, so we'll wait until after Lisa finishes singing and she can tell you the title herself. Lisa will be accompanied by her father, Mr. Henry Shin."

The audience applauded politely and Lisa and her father went onstage. As Mr. Faringhelli set the microphone for Lisa, I could see his hair and forehead shining with perspiration. As he came offstage, he wiped his face with both his hands and rubbed them on his jacket.

The audience was quiet as Mr. Shin, standing a little behind Lisa, looked at her a moment before he began to play. His eyes focused over his shoulder on his violin. His face went from looking as if he were holding an infant to looking very sad, as though he were in mourning for the child. Then as he played one long, deep note, Lisa's voice joined him in Korean, a language I'd never heard spoken, much less sung. But the beauty was in how their voices, his on violin and hers a high, birdlike soprano, joined together note for note. As they picked up speed, their moods seemed to change. Both of them smiled, and Lisa made a laughing, chirping sound that I couldn't imagine ever learning how to do.

Amber, who was standing in front of us, said, "I can't believe she's doing the whole thing in Korean. How does she expect anyone to vote for her if they can't even understand what she's singing?"

I felt Marcus put his hand on my shoulder to warn me, but I wouldn't have said anything anyway. I just closed my eyes and listened. *Center yourself, Lahni. And breathe.*

Mr. Faringhelli was on the other side of the stage now.

I could see him watching Lisa as she finished her song. It wasn't quite the same expression as when he played jazz on the piano with his eyes closed. It wasn't the expression he'd had when Marcus had tried out the piano, running his fingers up and down the keys, playing chords. But it was clear he was impressed with Lisa and her father's performance. He was proud of Lisa. I was happy for her and wanted the same for me.

I knew she was about to end when she repeated the same long phrase she'd begun with, only this time even higher and sweeter. Her face was as open as her voice sounded. Only her head tilted slightly upward as her hands remained at her sides, her arms hanging as though she had given herself up completely to the music.

There was definitely more than polite applause when she finished. The audience may not have understood what she was singing, but they knew she had a gorgeous voice. She was talented. Extremely talented. And they didn't need a translator to understand that.

Mr. Faringhelli ran out onstage, applauding. He went to the mic and said, "Lisa, that was incredible. You know, I told the audience rather than make a mistake trying to pronounce the title of the song, I'd ask you to do it. Would you tell us what it was?"

Lisa stepped closer to the microphone, and I realized

that the person I had just seen singing had vanished that quickly. Instead, a beautiful but very shy, nervous girl said something that no one heard. There was light applause, and Mr. Faringhelli looked like he was trying to decide whether to ask her to repeat it.

"I'm so glad I didn't try to say that myself," he said, and a few people laughed. "Thank you so much, Lisa. Ladies and Gentlemen, Lisa Shin, accompanied by her father, Mr. Henry Shin."

As Lisa came offstage toward us, Amber began vocalizing again. "Brrrrrr. Brrrrrrr. Ooo ahhh. Brrrrr." At the same time, she began pulling at her dress from every direction. She pulled it up, down, tugged at the bust, all the time blowing through her lips. "Brrrrrrr." And singing up and down the scale like she was being timed to see how fast it was humanly possible to do it. "Ooooo, aaaah, oooooo."

Lisa rushed by with her father. I managed to squeeze her arm and say, "Fantastic." Lisa smiled and thanked me. Her father was so excited, he thanked me three times in a row, and Marcus patted him on the back and said, "Well done, man. Well done."

"And here she is, our second performer for the evening, Amber Merrill." The applause was enormous. People were cheering. Amber flipped her hair and smoothed her dress. In a split second she went from tugging and oooing to being a finalist in the Miss Universe pageant. She waited for a moment before stepping onto the stage the way a champion diver might wait before flying headfirst into a pool. And while the audience was still applauding, Amber glided out onto the stage so smoothly, I could barely see her feet move under her gown.

When she got to center stage, she smiled at the audience like she knew how long they'd waited to see her and she wanted them to know she wouldn't disappoint them. She put her hands up, and I held my breath, realizing she was actually going to speak. The audience quieted obediently, and Amber purred, "Good evening. I'm so happy to be here. I know I'm not supposed to say anything before I sing. . . ."

Oh my God, I thought, *what's she going to do?* I looked at Mr. Faringhelli, who was sitting at the piano waiting to play for her. His face was pale, and he had both hands on the piano top, gripping it like it was a mountain cliff.

"But I realized"—and here Amber struck a 'terrified' pose—"Mr. Faringhelli forgot to announce the name of my song. And it's in English so I'm sure he can pronounce it." The audience laughed, not a huge laugh, but a friendly one. Mr. Faringhelli put his head down, playing along with being singled out as a goof-up, but now his face was red and I felt sorry for him.

"So . . . well, I decided to tell you myself," Amber continued, smiling sweetly. "I am going to sing a song tonight from the wonderful Broadway musical *The Loveliest Girl in the World.* The name of the song is—what else?—"'The Loveliest Girl in the World.'" And with that, Amber swung her hips from side to side as she simultaneously tossed her hair again. The audience laughed with delight and applauded. *Well, here we go,* I thought. Again, I felt Marcus put his hand on my shoulder. I turned to him, and he smiled at me. "Center yourself, little sister."

It went about as well as I expected. Amber also was talented. Watching her was an entirely different experience from watching Lisa, but I had to admit there was no question. Amber had a great voice and boy, was she ever a performer!

Sure, she did a couple of things I wouldn't have done. When she sang, "You make me feel like I've been waiting all my life," she tapped her foot and pretended to look at her watch. And she never sang the word "you" without pointing to the audience. But you could tell the audience loved her, and if *they* were deciding, she'd probably have won before the song was half over.

Before the song *was* half over, I stopped listening. At least to Amber. There was another voice in my head. *Now what are you going to do? You can't back out now. Do you realize how many people you could disappoint? Your mother, your father, Marcus, Mr. Faringhelli, Carietta, Katie, the members of the choir. C'mon, Lahni. Your voice is okay, but you're no Carietta. What are you doing competing?*

This time I wished it were as easy as feeling nauseous, as vomiting even, right there backstage. But it wasn't. I'd started to sweat. My whole body was clammy. Under my arms, under my dress. My hair was damp, my giant Afro felt like it *was* a wig I wanted to take off so my head would be cooler.

From what sounded like miles away, I could hear Amber singing her big finish. She held her last note for about an hour. The audience went wild. Screaming. Cheering. I could hear lots of kids' voices now. Donna had probably arranged a whole cheering section for Amber.

Mr. Faringhelli had told us that no matter what happened, we were not to go back onstage for another bow. He must have suspected if he didn't make a rule, Amber would be going back and forth endlessly. She practically tripped over me coming offstage without taking her eyes off the audience. "Did you hear that? I can't believe it. Did you hear that?"

I was just about to take a sip of water. "Congratulations, Amber. You were great."

I stood up and felt like I was on the way back down again. But I grabbed the back of the chair with one hand

and felt my hair with the other. I'd thought maybe my Afro had shrunk because I'd perspired so much, but it still felt pretty high. The combs were still in place. I saw that there were big perspiration stains under my arms, though, and even the neck and front of my dress were damp and dark. I certainly didn't have any lip gloss left on. Still, I said to Mr. Faringhelli, "I'm ready." I looked at Marcus. "Aren't we?"

"Yes, we are, little sister."

Mr. Faringhelli said to me very quietly, "Good luck, Lahni," and ran onstage.

Behind me, Amber hissed, "He didn't say that to anybody else."

"Our final performer tonight will be Lahni Schuler. She will be accompanied on piano by Marcus Delacroix III."

The cheers I heard when Mr. Faringhelli called my name were not as loud as the ones when Amber's name was called, but at least they were louder than the voice I'd heard in my head, backstage, telling me I was nuts to go onstage at all.

I went out first and Marcus came behind me. I felt more self-conscious than I ever remembered. I knew my dress looked like I'd already worn it some place else that night. I wondered if I'd walked onstage like my shoes were too tight. While my eyes got accustomed to the stage light, I tried hard to concentrate on what Marcus had told me. "Take your time. Get yourself together."

I heard the opening chords for our song. Marcus was making the keys say to me, *Come on, little sister. We've got something we're supposed to be doing out here.*

I started to hum. As soon as I did, my arms went up and folded themselves over my chest. I hadn't planned it. I'd planned to let them rest as gently and easily as Lisa's, so that I looked peaceful like the words of the song said I was. But, at that moment, I didn't feel faint or sick to my stomach or even nervous, but I didn't feel peaceful.

With my arms folded over my chest, I continued to hum. I told myself, *Lahni, as soon as you can, take your arms down. You want to look confident. You want to look like you know you're being watched over, taken care of.* But for then, I held myself, and the tighter I did, the more sadness filled me and I let it. I could hear the sadness, too, in Marcus's playing. He understood what I was feeling.

> "Why should I feel discouraged?
> Why should the shadows fall?
> Why should my heart feel lonely
> And long for heaven and home?"

I felt foolish in my sweaty silk dress and my tight shoes. I wanted to go home, put on my jeans, do homework again, and ride my bike. Most of all, I didn't want to be scared anymore. Scared about my parents. Scared that a divorce might destroy my mother and make my father a man I didn't want to see anymore. Scared I'd grow up mean and nasty like Onyx 1 because I didn't want to be who I really was.

"When Jesus is my portion
A constant friend is he
His eye is on the sparrow
And I know he watches me.
I sing because I'm happy"

I didn't feel happy at all, but I wanted to be.

"I sing because I'm free"

I didn't feel free either, but I wanted to be.

"Oh, His eye is on the sparrow
And I know He watches me."

Marcus played alone for a verse like we'd rehearsed. I looked out into the darkness of the auditorium. Suddenly I got a picture of myself outside in the parking lot, down on the concrete hearing Onyx 1 tell me he wondered if

I was one hundred percent black. And being so mad I forgot about being scared.

I saw myself getting up in his face knowing in that moment *exactly* who I was. I wasn't afraid because I knew I was protected, I felt so sure that I was.

That same feeling of sureness started to fill me again and I felt my arms relax and slowly fall to my sides. *His eye is on the sparrow. Yes, his eye is oooooonnnnnn the spaaarrooow!* And I was the sparrow. I'd been watched over in the parking lot. Mom and I had been watched over when we walked away from Dad's car in New York. I'd probably even been watched over when Mom and Dad decided it was me they wanted to take home knowing of course that I was brown and had fuzzy hair and somebody had already said they didn't want me. I was the sparrow. *And I knoooooowww He watches me.*

I was somewhere else, flying way over the auditorium, over the parking lot, when I heard them. The audience. They were clapping and I hadn't finished singing yet. I had one more line to sing, one more *And I know he watches me.* I wanted to take my time, to make it last as long as I had breath. Even though I could hear them clapping, I didn't stop flying. I didn't want to come down. Marcus knew it. He was playing like I'd never heard him play before. If I was flying, he was right beside me, smiling and nodding. *Sing, little sister, sing.*

Then it was over. I never came back down. I just finished the song from up where we were, me and Marcus. The applause was louder. I kept my eyes closed. I wanted us to stay where we were. I heard Marcus from over at the piano. "All right, little sister. We did what we came to do."

I opened my eyes. Marcus came toward me. I walked right into him and held on to him. My whole body was shaking. I was wet, he was drenched in perspiration, but I wanted to be there with him for a moment, because of where we'd been together. He put his hand on the back of my head and I held myself back from crying. I turned out to the audience. They were standing and yelling, cheering. I saw my mother's face, then my father's. He had his arm around her, and she was crying and calling my name. Marcus took my hand and we walked offstage and across the hall.

"Marcus?" I leaned into him, trying to keep it private. "It was so strange. But wonderful. I went somewhere else. I felt like *we* went somewhere else. Was I all right?"

Marcus stopped. He slid his glasses down his nose so I could see his eyes. "All right? Tonight, little sister, you sang the song. You hear me? You sang. The song."

Marcus stood back and let me go into the classroom first. As I passed him, he whispered. "And Marcus Delacroix could not be more proud."

We went into the classroom. Lisa and her father, Mr. Shin, were there. Even though we'd all been told that no visitors could be anywhere backstage until the decision had been announced, Amber and both of her parents were there. Mr. and Mrs. Merrill stared at me and neither of them said anything. I'd never met them, so I suppose I expected one of them to introduce themselves. I was, after all, in their daughter's class. But it didn't happen, and apparently that was fine with Amber.

Lisa came up to me and said, "You were so good, Lahni. I don't know who's going to win, but you were so good."

"Thanks, Lisa." I hugged her. "That was great. Your voice is gorgeous. I didn't know you spoke Korean."

Lisa giggled. "Are you kidding? I'm having enough trouble with Spanish One. My father taught me that song phonetically. At first I didn't even know what I was singing. But I heard it on a record and wanted to try it."

Mr. Faringhelli came into the classroom and went directly over to Mr. and Mrs. Merrill. "I'm really sorry. No visitors are supposed to be backstage until after the whole thing is over. I hope you don't mind. They're serving refreshments outside while the judges deliberate."

Mrs. Merrill picked up an embroidered shawl from the desk she'd been standing next to. "We didn't see what difference it made at this point."

Mr. Faringhelli nodded patiently. "I know. And it *is* almost over. It's just that we made the rule. So I kind of have to enforce it for everybody. I'm sorry."

He never talked to us students like that. He talked to us like we were practically adults. He was speaking to the Merrills like they were both bad puppies. Even though he'd asked them to leave—after they'd already known they shouldn't be there—Mrs. Merrill was still stalling. I couldn't remember exactly the line my father used about apples not falling far from the trees they came from, but I knew this was a perfect example.

Mr. Merrill had been sitting at one of the kids' desks. "Come on Gina, honey. Amber will be okay."

Amber shook her hair and said loudly, "Me? I'm fine. I didn't tell you guys to come in here. Don't get Mr. Faringhelli pissed at *me*!"

Mrs. Merrill glared at Amber. They started to leave. Mrs. Merrill stopped in front of me and Marcus. "Was that what you'd call a spiritual?"

"I—I—I'm not sure," I stammered. And I wasn't. I just knew it was a song Marcus had picked for the choir, and I'd chosen to sing it for the competition. Still, I felt dumb saying I didn't know. I thought Marcus would answer her, but he didn't.

"I think so. I think that's what they call a spiritual,"

Mrs. Merrill said to me as though she felt sorry for me not knowing what the heck I was singing. "Very pretty."

As soon as they were gone, Mr. Faringhelli said, "I've got to go out to the auditorium now to wait for the judges' decision. It should take only a few minutes. I'll be back to get you and bring you onstage." He got to the door and turned around. "You all did a great job. I'm proud of all of you."

For a few minutes, we sat in absolute silence. We could hear the audience down the hall, waiting for the intermission to be over so they could find out the winners. Some of the Darby girls who knew where we were passed by our classroom door and waved. A few said "hi" or "good luck," mostly to Amber, but a couple to me and Lisa, too. I was hoping Katie would come by. I knew she had to be in the audience, and I wished one of the students would come especially to see me, even if they couldn't stay.

Mr. Shin went out to the men's room, and Marcus sat down with a whole package of about thirty chocolate chip cookies and a big bottle of Diet Pepsi. I took my heels off and wriggled my toes. They were throbbing.

Amber got up and went to pour herself a cup of water. She sat and took out her mascara. "You know, I hate to say this, but I really think this part is a waste of time."

Everyone in the room stared in her direction.

"I mean, don't you think they know already? They knew as soon as we all finished. What is there to talk about really? Don't you know right away if you like something or not?"

Amber stood up. Everything in her purse spilled out all over the floor, but she ignored it. "Well, I think it's the truth, even if no one else will admit it."

Marcus said, "I think I'll wait outside in the hallway, little sister. You wanna come along?"

I would have, except I wasn't sure I could get my shoes back on easily. "I'll be right out," I told him. I started easing my feet back into my heels a little at a time.

Maybe Amber had been right. Mr. Faringhelli seemed to be back much sooner than I'd thought. "The judges have made their decision, and it's time for all of you to go back onstage to hear the announcement."

Amber sighed loudly, gathering her things from the floor. "Told you. They knew as soon as we were done."

We all filed across the hall to the auditorium. Mr. Faringhelli, Amber, Mr. Shin, Lisa, Marcus, and me. We went to the center of the stage in one line as Mr. Faringhelli went up to the microphone.

"I want to say that The Darby School is proud of all three of these girls. It sounds so corny to say that they are all winners, but they are. You saw how talented each of them is. Didn't you?"

The audience applauded. I still, for some reason, could not look out into it. I focused on the back wall instead.

"I want to remind the audience of who our judges are tonight. They are Harry Klapson, Myrna Shwartzchild, and our special guest judge, Mrs. Daisy Clarke, the wife of our mayor." Light, polite applause from the audience.

"And now," Mr. Faringhelli continued, "I want to reintroduce you to the three girls you heard sing." He looked back at us for a second and said, "I'm going to ask the girls to come forward and for their accompanists to remain where they are, please."

I looked at Marcus. He looked over his glasses at me and nodded very slowly. *Thank you, God,* I thought, *for Marcus. Thanks for letting him be my friend.*

Lisa, Amber, and I all stepped forward. There were some whistles and calling out of "Yay, Amber!" Then a couple of people, Katie being one of them, yelled, "Go, Lahni!" and a couple more shouted, "Lisa!" I wanted Mr. Faringhelli to get on with it because this part was embarrassing. It felt more like a popularity contest than it had before.

"Mrs. Clarke, may I ask you to come up, please, and give us the name of the winner?"

The mayor's wife, in a boxy orange suit, left the long table the judges were sitting at and came toward the stage. As she crossed in front of the audience, I got another glimpse of my parents. Seeing them sitting there together, I honestly thought I didn't care what happened after that.

Then I saw their expressions. They were both looking at me as though I were five and about to jump out of a tree in the backyard. I hoped I didn't have the same look on my face as they did. I was trying to look like I might have a chance. They looked to me like they thought it would take a miracle for the mayor's wife to call my name.

Mr. Faringhelli went to the side of the stage to help Mrs. Clarke up. She had an index card in her hand, and I thought, *She only has one name to say. What does she need a whole index card for?*

"You know," Mr. Faringhelli told the audience, "I just realized how nervous *I* am. I'm a wreck!" The audience laughed and applauded.

By the time Mrs. Clarke got to the center of the stage, I felt like I'd been running for ten miles nonstop. I was practically panting and yet so filled with energy I could have run ten miles more. I wanted to take Mrs. Clarke in her orange suit and swing her around in circles—then grab that silly white index card from her hands and scream whatever name was on it seventy-five times just so that it would be over.

Mr. Faringhelli guided Mrs. Clarke over to the microphone and said, "Mrs. Clarke, would you read the name of the winner, please?"

Mrs. Clarke turned to us—and I swear I was fighting the urge to grab her for a do-si-do. She said, "First of all, I want to tell all three of you that you were marvelous. All, marvelous." Then she shook hands with each of us—which made it even harder to resist grabbing both of hers.

She turned back to the microphone and said, "Don't you agree?" to the audience. More applause.

When I wanted to scream out, *Please, Jesus, please let her read the name, already!* Mrs. Clarke read from her white index card.

"The winner of The Darby School talent competition is Lahni Schuler."

I used to hear people say they didn't remember a whole lot after a moment like that, and I thought they were lying. I didn't know why they'd lie. I just couldn't believe they wouldn't remember every single detail of something like that. But now I know. When I tell people I don't remember much after hearing my name, I'm not lying at all.

What I do remember is Lisa hugging me and Mr. Faringhelli hugging me too, but I don't remember how I got off the stage and into the audience. Did Marcus carry me off? Probably not. But he was there, and I definitely don't have any memory of walking.

I know Carietta got to me before anyone else, mashed my head into her breasts, and held her hands over my ears so hard I thought I'd gone deaf.

"Ohmygodohmygod! I can't believe it!" Katie kept saying, and laughing hysterically. It was like a chorus playing over the PA.

I have pictures of my parents in the school hallway with their arms around me. Sometimes I look at them and think we almost look like a happy family.

When we all got to the back entrance of the school, I stood in the doorway, looking out into the parking lot. That's the first moment after Mrs. Clarke announced my name that I do remember very distinctly. I was holding the little gold trophy in my hand and watching all the car lights turn on in the dark. I could hear the voices of people telling me how well I'd sung. There were so many members of the choir, we could've had a rehearsal right there.

My father was saying he had to get back to the city because he was leaving the next morning for Germany. I looked at him and felt a sharp pain go through my body. More than anything in the world, I wanted to go home with both my parents and celebrate with pistachio ice cream and brownies. But just that fast, my father was disappearing into the parking lot, and I knew they had come in separate cars to make this part easier for them.

I recognized somebody else in the parking lot too. Even though I saw him from behind, I knew right away who it was. He had on a cap, tilted to the side, and a pair of really wide jeans with Day-Glo graffiti on them. Hanging onto him was some girl I didn't recognize in a sweatshirt with the hood covering her head. The two of them got into his Toyota and drove off. Was I surprised that he'd shown up? I couldn't say really. But it didn't matter anymore what he did. As long as he kept his distance.

Right next to me, Marcus and Carietta were imitating me sing. Marcus sang a long, high note and said, "Now, you know nobody *ever* heard her do *that* before!"

Carietta said, "I know I got my work cut out for me if I'm gonna keep singing next to Miss Lahni."

My mother was holding my hand and asking me where I wanted to go to celebrate. Her eyes said, *I hope you know this is the best I could do.* I kissed her on the cheek and whispered that I loved her.

Then, very slowly, in bits and pieces, I started to really

understand what had just happened to me. Tonight, I thought, on that stage with Marcus playing beside me, I wasn't really singing at all. I was praying. Praying not to be afraid. That God's eye really could be on a sparrow. That whatever was to happen with my parents would go ahead and happen and that, like Marcus said, we really would be okay. All of us.

And that the girl my mother told me she saw when she looked at me would be the same girl I saw when I looked at myself. A black girl named Lahni Schuler. And that would be okay too. Better than okay.

And I actually think God heard me. Not because of the trophy. But because by the time I finished singing, I had my answer.

Tomorrow, or next week, when there aren't any fuchsia lights and there's no audience watching, no silk dress or giant Afro, and Marcus isn't playing the piano like he does, I might have to pray again. I might have to ask again if I really am worth God keeping his eye on me. And all I can do, I guess, is hope the answer will still be yes.